ALL I HEAR IS BANJOS

The Balllad of a Simple Man

Caleb Smith

First and foremost, I'd like to thank my wife for her long-suffering patience and ever present kindness. I love you dearly, more than you'll ever know. Secondly, I want to thank you, the reader. Without you, I wouldn't be allowed to continue doing what I love; writing about doing stupid things.

PREFACE

Here we go again. Another volume jam packed full of my adventures (and misadventures). All of the stories here are 100% true, except for the ones that arent. If you enjoy this book, please take a moment to head over to Amazon and leaving a review. It really helps me out.

I hope you enjoy.

TAKE IT TO THE LIMIT

◆ ◆ ◆

Writing is hard.

There's the whole problem of crafting a story; creating a cohesive tale with a beginning, middle, and end. Most people can start a story, and a few people can make the middle, but very few people can build a satisfying end. No one enjoys a story without an end or, as I like to call it, a conversation with my boss.

Then there's grammar, sentence structure, and spelling, and don't get me started on punctuation.

Oh, how I hate punctuation.

For all this hard work, you would think that it came with equal rewards. What I'm about to say may shock many of you, but a humor columnist on page four of a small-town newspaper doesn't exactly live a life of luxury.

So why do we do it? Why do we struggle with the English language with all of its foibles and hairpin twists and turns? Why do we put ourselves out there, exposing ourselves to ridicule and mockery for absolutely no return? The answer is pretty simple.

We're all a little bit crazy.

Writers are, as my carpenter dad would say, all about a half bubble off plumb. Those that live in the South will understand when I say, about all writers, 'Bless their hearts'.

Once you get past grammar and actually creating a good story, you also have to meet certain standards when you're writing for a reputable paper. You can't be too offensive, can't be too controversial, and, worst of all, you have to meet a certain word count.

For me, it's 450 words.

Do you have any idea how hard it is to encapsulate my daily idiocy into just 450 words? When I began writing for the paper, my editor told me 'It's ok if you can't come up with something every week. It can be hard to have something interesting happen to write about that frequently.'

Little did he realize that the problem would not be to find dumb things I've done to write about, it would be to pick out *which* dumb thing I've done to write about.

I could write 450 words a *day* about the stupid things I've done, and still not run out. But that's what I've been told I have to, keep it short.

The more I think about it, the more it raises my hackles. Who is my editor to limit how many words I can write? 450 words are too few, I can't limit it that much. I'm going to make a stand; Mr. Editor, I'm going to write until I finish my story, who gives you the right to cut me off. What are you going to do about it, take your pen and....

THE SIX DOLLAR MAN

◆ ◆ ◆

As you begin to get older, it's not uncommon for your senses to begin to fail. I first noticed there was something wrong with my hearing a couple of years back. I kept hearing a popping, cracking noise wherever I went. Chalking it up to years of hunting and firearm practice without proper hearing protection, I told my wife I was going to consult with a doctor about it.

"There's nothing wrong with your hearing," she said as she cleaned up the Twinkie wrappers scattered around my desk. "Those are your joints."

To say that I was dismayed would be an understatement. While to my mind I am still a young, vibrant, virile man, my body apparently has other ideas. While once 'Snap, crackle, pop' was merely the slogan of my favorite cereal, now it's the theme music anytime I get up from my armchair.

Sleeping on the wrong side has become an extreme sport now, one where I wake up aching and sore. Tylenol has become my breakfast of choice. Little things that used to not bother me; sports, working in the yard, bending over slightly, now threaten to put me on the couch for a week with a sprained back.

I have only myself to blame. Since getting married I have not led the most active life. A combination of my wife's excellent cooking and a sedentary job has given me a 'dad bod' long before fatherhood. I'm so out of shape, I'm the only person I know that sweats from bowling, a sport that is literally sitting and waiting your turn 90% of the time.

It's not just my body that's going to seed either, my mind is starting to slip too. A few weeks ago I turned the house upside down looking for my lost pair of glasses. I had a hard time seeing so I had to pull my glasses out of my shirt pocket to help me look.

It took me over an hour to realize my mistake.

The worst part was my wife actually helped me look for them.

Long time T.V. watchers will remember Lee Majors as the Six Million

Dollar Man, a soldier wounded so grievously they had to rebuild him using the full resources of the federal government. In my case I feel like I was rebuilt will Dollar Store discount items.

We have the technology, we just don't have the funding.

Unfortunately, I just don't see it getting much better. I have accepted my state of mental and physical and have decided to enjoy the twilight years of my life with as much grace and dignity as I can muster. I suppose it was just a matter of time, after all, I turn 31 in a few months. How much mental or physical acuity can someone expect when they're that ancient?

SUSPICIOUS MINDS

◆ ◆ ◆

With so much time spent at home these days, I quickly began to run out of things to do. I've watched Netflix (all of it), read every book in the house, and taken apart every appliance we have in order to 'make them more efficient'. After the third time, I was left with spare parts after reassembling an appliance, my wife firmly put her foot down, thus depriving me of another creative outlet.

Out of boredom, and a healthy fear of what my wife would do to me if I didn't do something other than nap on the couch all day, I decided to give Podcasts a try.

Podcasts, for those who are unfamiliar, are basically radio shows that you can download off the internet and listen to on your phone. The first time I signed in, I was immediately overwhelmed at the offerings. There were literally had tens of thousands of hours of every type show imaginable. Comedies, dramas, history lessons, and politics all just waiting to be listened to.

My favorite of all, however, was the murder podcasts.

True Crime is a popular subject on any form of media; television, movies, or books, and Podcasts were no different. There were hundreds of unique channels, all dedicated to telling gruesome tales of individuals who had all they could take of their loved ones, and turned on them. It was a testament to the twisted and convoluted nature of the human mind.

And then I started noticing things around the house.

It started small at first. A wet spot on the floor that I slipped on, forks placed in the sink upside down with the tines pointed up, simple things that could have been chalked up to mere happenstance.

Then bigger things started happening.

I opened the door to my pantry the other day and was nearly brained as a can of beans rolled off the top shelf, narrowly missing my head.

"Oh dear," My wife said calmly, "Did you almost get hit? How lucky it missed."

As I lay in bed that night, I began to wonder, had it really been an accident? All these years I thought I was just brash and clumsy, a combination that lends itself to occasional mishaps, but what if everything had been planned? What if, every time I accidently set the yard on fire, or electrocuted myself, or smashed my thumb with a hammer, what if they had all been attempts on my life.

What if my wife had had enough of me, *just like in the murder podcasts.*

As I got ready to go to sleep, I grabbed my cover and pulled it up. As I did so, my hand slipped and I punched myself in the face.

I slept soundly that night, secure in the realization that my wife wasn't trying to kill me.

I really am just that clumsy.

ONCE A PUN A TIME

◆ ◆ ◆

Puns are, without a doubt, the absolute lowest form of humor. They are lazy, dumb, empty jokes that primarily appeal to the lowest of intellects.

So of course, I absolutely love them.

I love puns so much, I will go out of my way just to set up a good pun. I once drove all the way to town, went to the grocery store and bought a package of leeks from the produce section. I went home and quickly set about putting my plan into action.

My task accomplished, I came stomping into the house, swearing and shaking my head.

"What's wrong dear?" My wife asked as she looked up from cooking dinner.

"Ah, it's the roof. We've got half a dozen leeks."

"Oh no!" She raced over to the door, "Where at? Show me."

We walked out into the yard and I grimly pointed to the produce I had thrown on top of the house.

"See?" I said, trying not to laugh. "Look at all the leeks."

If you've never seen an overweight man running through the yard, giggling madly while his wife chases him with a spatula, you're missing out. It's a pretty common sight in our neighborhood.

You think she would have learned after I laid all the coffee mugs on the lawn and came in, loudly complaining about how *muggy* it was outside.

Most people don't have to go to all that effort for a good pun. If you know where to look, puns are all around us. I remember as a child, I was helping my mother in the garden one day. Seeing my opportunity, I grabbed a handful of green beans up and asked her, "Hey mama, how have you *bean*?" She just rolled her eyes.

I quickly darted over to the corn, "Sorry, was that joke too *corny*?" Her lips pressed tight as she kept picking.

"Hey watch out for that snake," I said, pointing at the cucumbers she was picking.

"That doesn't even make sense." She snapped at me, "These don't even sound lik- *a snake!*"

After we coaxed her down from the tree, I was grounded and forbidden from ever making puns again. For years I abided by those rules.

And then I got married, and the real fun started.

Not long after we got our first house, my wife and I were in the hardware store and she reminded me that I still needed to sow our yard with grass.

"Well, I'll try my best." I said, scratching my head dubiously, "But I don't know if they sell needles here."

My new bride rolled her eyes, an expression I soon became very familiar with.

Some people just don't appreciate a good pun.

WASTED DAYS AND WASTED NIGHTS

Time loses all meaning when you're working from home. Pajamas are business attire, brushing your hair is an unnecessary luxury, and the return of the mountain man style beard and the mullet now seems inevitable.

The world has turned into the opening scenes from a disaster movie. The worst part is, it doesn't look like it would be a very good movie either. Newspaper headlines call for mass hysteria, and chaos and pandemonium are now the order of the day.

But let's talk about me some more.

The days on the calendar are losing all relevance as time ticks by. When every day consists of sitting in front of a keyboard, snacking, before moving to your recliner to rewatch old Buffy the Vampire Slayer reruns (and more snacking) what does it matter if it's a Monday or a Friday?

Nothing is more demoralizing than to work all day, looking forward to 5 PM and clocking out for the weekend, only to realize it's just Monday.

On the other hand, all day last Friday I was convinced it was Monday. My wife had to show me the calendar on her phone that evening to convince me I didn't have to go to work the next day. That was a nice surprise.

At this point in my life, my day to day activities have been reduced to sitting in front of different sized screens (computer vs.

T.V.) and endlessly snacking.

Which is not as big of a departure from my normal life as you might think.

We've all been turned into Ariel from The Little Mermaid; wistfully looking at a world barred to us as we longingly sing 'Part of Your World', only in our case we're singing about going to a restaurant or just leaving the house.

And no, I never thought I would be comparing myself to the Little Mermaid.

The best thing we can do is to pick up hobbies around the house to keep ourselves entertained. Since I have such a love of eating, I thought I might enjoy taking up cooking. My kitchen privileges were speedily revoked, however, the first time I set fire to the microwave.

How was I supposed to know you can't bypass the grilling process by simply nuking a steak for an hour? They should really include that in the instructions.

After this ill-fated venture, I decided to stick with testing different snack food combinations, but I quickly had to give that up due to health concerns.

By the way, don't try wrapping an Airhead around a Slim-Jim and calling it a pig in a blanket. It's delicious, but the gastric distress isn't worth the novelty of the snack.

BREAD AND WHINE

◆ ◆ ◆

Another day, another diet. After I broke another office chair, I decided to sit down (well ok, I was already on the ground) and get down to the business of losing weight. After extensive research, where I marked out the diets I've already tried, I was left with only one.

Low carb, sugar-free.

This was last on my list as it was the most difficult one for me to tackle. Sugar makes up approximately 80% of my diet (and 40% of my blood according to recent lab work, doctors are still looking into it). Giving up such a large part of my personality was going to be hard, but I owed it to my wife.

She was tired of buying new chairs.

The diet started out easily enough, low carb meant I got to eat all the meat that I want. As a lifelong carnivore, this was music to my ears. I started out by having 3 boiled eggs and a pound of bacon for breakfast.

I have never felt healthier than when I was slowly munching my way through a mound of greasy pork. Best diet ever.

Things quickly spiraled out of control when I asked for pasta.

"No can do," my wife said as she scrubbed at the bacon grease that had somehow made it onto the walls. "Full of gluten. I'm making you some nice, gluten-free, low carb meals from now on."

I'm not a particularly educated man. I have a couple of degrees under my belt, but biology was never one of my strong suits. As such, I'm not entirely sure what carbs are or how they can contribute to weight gain, all I can say is that carbs are apparently what give food their flavor.

Sugar was doubly hard to give up. I have given up nicotine (dozens of times now) and the withdrawals from the devil's plant are nothing compared to sugar withdrawals. I spent days in a cold sweat, curled up under the desk in my office. My wife would leave my meals at the door, then withdraw, leaving me to reach one pale hand outside my dark cave and snatch the plate of bland gruel. I would scurry back into my room, eating it with my bare hands while I wistfully thought of candy bars, cokes, and cotton candy.

That had always made the best breakfast.

Finally, weeks later, the worst of the symptoms passed and I was able to emerge back into civilized society. I approached the scale, excited to see just how much weight I had lost during the torturous experience.

The digital display blinked and showed me my numbers.

I had gained 3 pounds.

EXERCISE OR EXTRA FRIES?

◆ ◆ ◆

I've always had a little bit of extra padding around the middle. Not necessarily fat, I was what most people would call 'husky' or 'big-boned'. Being stuck at home for the past few months hasn't helped that in the least. My wife, either out of a desire to see me happy or as part of a calculated plan to collect my life insurance money when I collapse face first in my biscuits and gravy, has made sure that all of my favorite snacks and foods are well-stocked for the duration of the quarantine.

The problem with this is that my favorite foods are all chock full of sugars and trans-fats and all the other things scientists are saying are bad for us. My average diet would be considered a violation of the Geneva convention if it were forced on prisoners of war.

The end result is that my weight has ballooned over the past few months. Now people use adjectives like 'jolly' or 'Santa Clause-esque' or (unkindly) 'like a pig stood up on its back legs and grew a beard'.

Something had to change.

So I decided to go on a diet. It seems like every month I'm trying out a new one only to quickly give it up. All diets have the same problem, there's never enough food!

Finally, I found a loophole; you just need to go on two or three diets at the same time. One diet allows bread, another diet allows cheese. Try both diets at the same time and you can have it all.

Honestly, I'm surprised more people haven't caught on to this little trick.

It makes logical sense too. If one diet will help you lose 10 pounds a month, then two diets should help you lose 20! It's just simple math.

After I fixed the problem of food, I had to make some decisions about exercise. Leaping to conclusions, running my mouth, and pushing people away doesn't burn as many calories as you might think, so I had to come up with an incentive to haul myself out of my chair and start sweating.

The solution, as is so often the case, presented itself in my wife. After a bit of ingenuity, not to mention persuasion, I finally rigged up a reward system for myself. My wife would sit on the couch with a fishing pole with a donut at the end of the line. I would then have her raise and lower the donut as I did pushups, my head following the treat.

Unfortunately, these sessions always devolved into me laying on my back and pawing at the donut like a cat, so it's back to the drawing board again.

MAN ON THE RUN

◆ ◆ ◆

I like to think I'm a pretty accepting guy. I give everyone the benefit of the doubt regardless of color, creed, or criminal history. I pride myself on the fact that I withhold judgment of someone until I get to know them for myself. No matter who you are, know that you and I will always start off with a blank slate.

Unless you're a jogger.

Psychopaths.

This is the time of year I park my car as close to the house as possible, and I always use my remote start to make sure the air in my vehicle is running for a good ten minutes before I venture out. When I'm ready to leave, I'll make a mad dash for the car (or at least the slow, shambling shuffle that passes for a mad dash with me) to limit my time spent outside as much as possible.

Georgia is almost uninhabitable for 8 months out of the year, especially so during the spring. It's blazing hot, filled with biting, stinging, buzzing insects that seem to harbor a deep-seated hatred for all of humanity. Ant that's not even mentioning the humidity. Georgia is so muggy, it's the only state where the mosquitoes have to wear water wings in order to stay aloft. It's the type of torture that most first world countries have banned under human rights legislation.

Despite all that, this man was willingly out and about, jogging.

My first reaction was, there must be a bear chasing him. Nothing else that I could think of would incite me to run in the middle of the day during a Georgia springtime, and even then I wouldn't subject myself to it for long before laying down and giving up to the bear. Some things are worse than death.

The man showed no signs of distress was I passed however, even smiling and throwing me a friendly little wave.

I just glared suspiciously at him until I was passed.

Not only was he jogging for recreation, but he also seemed to be *enjoying* it.

It's terrifying to me that these people exist among us, un-known and unseen unless caught in the act. Your neighbor could be a jogger, the person that sits beside you at church could be one. Your own spouse could be part of their number, and you might never know until its too late.

I understand why they do it, the health benefits are clear and irrefutable. I'm all for extending my time on Earth for as long as the good Lord will let me stay here, but at what *cost?* Anyone who has ever eaten a value sized box of gas station sushi will tell you; sometimes it's more about quality than quantity.

A MISERY OF RICHES

◆ ◆ ◆

Gardens. Some love them, some hate them. Even though I have not willingly eaten a vegetable in years, I decided to plant one back in the spring. Initially, all went well. The time spent weeding, watering, and fertilizing it was just the sort of calming activity I needed to help decompress from the stress of the world.

Recently, however, things have taken a dark turn.

The garden began to bear fruit.

It started slow. First, the lettuce began to mature. "No big deal," I thought to myself, "I have friends that like lettuce, I'll give it away." But it kept growing. What appeared to be a small, compact growth of leaves actually turned out to be a densely packed nightmare, each plant yielding more lettuce than the average family consumes in a year.

A visitor to my home this past weekend would have found me in the kitchen, feverishly packing grocery bags full of freshly washed lettuce. A keen observer may have noticed a slightly manic gleam in my eye or nervous sweat upon my brow. The lettuce soon filled my fridge and then overflowed into the rest of the house.

The pantry is full of lettuce, the kitchen cabinets are full of lettuce. I even went to get some cereal the other day, and lettuce came pouring out.

Eventually, I was able to get all of it picked and washed and stored away. I began to relax as I plucked the final plant. As I carried the last pail-full into the house, however, a glint of color caught my eye.

My squash plants had begun to bloom.

Grasping green tendrils have extended out, and I swear they're pointing right at the house, almost as though they're coming for me.

I hurriedly went inside and locked the door, drawing the blinds so the squash couldn't see me.

That night, I had a nightmare where I was laying in bed, sound asleep, when I heard a rapping at the window. In the dream, I got up and slowly pulled the curtain back to see what's causing the noise. There, on the other side of the window, was a squash vine, menacingly holding a switchblade. My screams of terror awakened my wife.

It was only after half an hour of reassurances from her that, no, the vegetables couldn't hurt me (a conversation we have every time she tries to get me to go on a diet) that I was able to drift back to sleep.

As I left for work the next day, I glanced towards the garden and stopped as a wave of dread washed over me.

The squash was still growing.

And the vines were even closer to the house this time.

APOCALYPSE COW

◆ ◆ ◆

Growing up, I always loved westerns. John Wayne, Clint Eastwood, Roy Rogers; all men that I looked up to and admired. Like most kids, I had a cowboy hat and a pair of toy-six shooters. My cousins and I used to love to play Cowboys and Indians (this was before the PC police got involved and it was changed to Colonialists and Indigenous Peoples, a much less fun game). When I wasn't playing that, I would swagger around like I was Doc Holiday, tipping my hat to my grandparents as I tried to wrangle the family cat.

As an aside, I highly recommend to any rodeos that may be reading that they incorporate Cat Wrangling into their next event. Riding a bucking bronco is exciting, but it can't hold a candle to what happens when a 5-year-old gets a noose around a 30-pound tabby.

So when I got married and discovered my new in-laws had an honest to goodness herd of cattle, I was delighted. Here was my chance to live out the fantasies of my youth. I dusted off my old hat (a bit small, but with a bit of string I was able to tie it to my head), slipped on a pair of boots, and grabbed a length of rope.

It was time to be a cowboy.

As I entered the pasture, I had to step gingerly to avoid the biological land mines that cattle are known to leave behind. I slowly approached one massive heifer, the rope held loosely in one hand. She gazed back at me with dull, uninterested eyes, as she placidly chewed at her cud. Feeling the spectral figures of the cowboys of yesteryear guiding my hand, I let the rope fly!

It sailed the 10 feet between us and bounced off the cow's side. I reeled it back in and tried again. And again.

And again.

On the fifth toss, the noose finally settled around the cow's neck. I enjoyed a moment of triumph before the cow reacted. She had watched my efforts up to this point with polite disinterest, but as soon as she felt the rope on her neck, she went insane. Bellowing, she kicked her feet and took off at a run. I stared stupidly from the cow, down to the coil of rope rapidly unspooling at my feet, and finally back to the rope I still held in my hand.

Before I could react, the slack was gone and the line went taut. I'm proud to say I managed to stay on my feet for several seconds. I must have looked something like a water-skier, my boots stuck out in front of me as the enraged cow pulled me through the pasture. Finally, however, I hit a bump and, after gaining an impressive amount of airtime, lost my balance and fell on my face. I was pulled several hundred more yards through the minefield of cattle droppings before finally letting the rope go.

When my wife asked me later why I held on that long, I just paused as I dramatically pulled my hat off, cattle dung falling from inside the crown.

"Well little lady," I said as I firmly set it back on my head, "I guess that's just what a good cowboy does."

JUST ME AND CHEW

◆ ◆ ◆

"I wish you would quit chewing tobacco." My wife sweetly said to me the other day. I calmly and rationally explained to her that, while on paper that might seem like a good idea, the physiological, as well as emotional effects of the immediate cessation of nicotine, could be detrimental to our marital bliss.

We had a rather spirited discussion about it, with her wanting me to stop immediately, cold turkey, and me arguing that I should at least taper off first. Both sides had excellent points that were well-argued, so we decided to compromise and that I would quit at once.

Cold turkey.

To those of you that don't know, tobacco was discovered in the New World by John Rolfe of Jamestown back in the 1600s. It was given to him by the local Indian tribe, a group who truly hated the white man. They saw how much trouble the Europeans were going to be over the next few centuries, so they introduced an addictive and deadly plant that would mess with the white man long after the tribe was gone. They were effective beyond their wildest dreams.

The Europeans took this Trojan Horse and gleefully ran with it. Throughout the years they discovered new and exciting ways of ingesting the plant. They figured out they could chew it, sniff it, and even smoke it. I maintain the greatest marketer that ever lived was the man who convinced people to stick a leaf in their mouth, set it on fire, and breathe in the smoke. Genius.

Now let me be clear, tobacco in any form is a filthy, disgusting, cancer-causing habit. Even more so with chewing tobacco. To give it up should have been the easiest, and best, decision of my life. Instead, it has been some of the worst torture I've ever had to endure.

Since giving up tobacco, I have steadily made my way through everything to eat in the house, worn out 3 fidget spinners, and chewed through more toothpicks than a beaver on a diet.

It's been 48 hours.

Last night was better, however, as I was actually able to sleep for thirty or forty minutes, two or three of which actually happened in a row. The rest of the night was spent staring at the ceiling while camels and grizzlies danced on the periphery of my vision.

Despite all that, I have remained as gentle and good-natured as always. I've only had 3 meltdowns over the past couple of days, which honestly is about average.

By and large, I know this is a good decision. It's best for my family, and it's best for me. I just need to buckle down, hold on tight, and maybe snack a little bit more.

If I can't chew tobacco, cake is the next best thing.

A CLEAR AND PRESENT HANGER

◆ ◆ ◆

I'm not a nice person when I'm hungry. I can turn from the nicest guy you've ever met, in Mr. Hyde if I miss a single meal. Now, having a body type that's usually reserved for marine mammal's, you would think that it's not often that I go hungry. I'm usually the first one to the dinner table and the last one to leave. But sometimes the unavoidable happens (my wife leaves for a weekend and the microwave is down, just for instance) and I don't get fed in a timely manner. Then disaster can strike.

My wife learned early in our marriage that the jovial, wise-cracking man she married would disappear if I went too long between meals, and a surly, hulking jerk would take his place. So she started stashing snacks at strategic points around the house.

She learned to watch for the signs; a furrowed brow, running my hand through my hair in exasperation, a low, furious rumble, and she would appear, Debbie Cake in hand. She would have to approach me like a tiger handler, crooning to me in a soft voice until I snatched the treat from her hand and she was able to pet me safely.

We were not always able to have snacks on hand, however. Adult life necessitates leaving the house sometimes (a fact for which I am actively searching for a loophole to), and sometimes we were left without any option other than to have to *gasp* wait to eat.

Usually, we were able to get to a fast food restaurant before I worked myself too far into a rage, but a couple of times we were too far out in the boonies to get to anywhere fast enough. She wound up dumping me on the side of the road and driving off.

I don't hold any hard feelings, she did what she had to do.

She's a smart woman, however, and was able to come up with a safety measure in case we ever find ourselves in a predicament like that again. Now we don't go anywhere without a case of coke, a pack of crackers, and a little holster she belts on to hold an emergency twinkie, just in case.

Working from home most of the week, my desk looks like ravenous raccoons broke into a vending machine. Candy wrappers and crumbs cover most of the desktop, a pile of crumpled coke cans fill a corner of the room. Every once in a while I'll see that I'm almost out of snacks. A low rumble of anger will fill the room, and shortly, another package of snacks will be thrown through my door.

My wife is a good woman.

THE QUICK AND
THE BREAD

◆ ◆ ◆

"And just where do you think you're going?" My wife said, hands on her hips.

I paused, my keenly attuned Husband Senses flashed a warning that danger was near. I decided to proceed with caution.

"I'm going fishing," I said, meekly holding up my rod by way of demonstration. "You look pretty today," I added as an after-thought.

"Fishing my right elbow." She spat grumpily. I was shocked. My wife normally doesn't resort to language that strong. "The yard looks like a jungle, the porch is falling apart, and you still haven't fixed that light bulb in the kitchen. I'm stuck cleaning and you're off galivanting on the lake somewhere. You're probably going to make me cook any fish you catch, aren't you?"

"Of course my, uh, my turtledove," I said, genuinely confused. "We both get to do things we enjoy. I get to go fishing, and you get to clean and cook and generally take care of me."

I did not get to go fishing that day.

When the tumult subsided, I was left holding a mop, an apron, and something called a 'toilet wand' while my wife went off to take a nap. Something about trading spaces for a day, but hon-estly, I hadn't paid much attention during all the yelling.

All I knew for certain were two things. 1: I had to have dinner ready when my wife woke up and 2: there is absolutely nothing magical about a toilet wand.

Now I don't know much about cooking....

There's no 'but' to that sentence. I don't know much about cooking. The end.

I finally decided on a simple dinner of homemade bread and tomato soup. How much easier could a meal get? The ingredients for tomato soup were right there in the name; tomatoes, and I figured if pilgrims could bake bread over a fire made out of buffalo chips, how hard could it be?

I plopped two whole tomatoes into a pot of water and set it to boil, then I set to making the bread. I threw together the flour and water only to discover that I had added too much water. So I added more flour. Only to find out that I needed to add a little bit more water. I repeated these steps several times until I had run through the entire bag of flour. I ladled the soupy mixture into several pans, then slid it into the oven.

Dusting the excess flour off my hands (and my shirt, and my hair, and the seat of my pants) I plopped down on the couch and flipped on the TV.

I must have been tuckered out from all that cooking because the smoke detector woke me up and an hour later.

I was very happy to treat my wife to a dinner out on the town that night.

TIME AFTER TIME

◆ ◆ ◆

It's a sad fact that I am afflicted with a perpetual case of poor timing. Everywhere I go I am either a little too early, or just a hair too late. Redlights always seem to turn red just as I come upon them. Popcorn always gets just a little too burnt. I always seem to show up to a store the day *after* they were running a sale on the item I was wanting to buy. All a case of poor timing.

No greater example presents itself to me than in the case of my garden. Let me explain. Every year in November I suit up in expensive camouflage and sneak off into the woods. I leave hours before dawn so I can arrive at my stand long before the sun rises. I sit perfectly still for hours on end, too afraid that if I so much as cough I will scare away the deer.

Finally, around lunchtime, hunger will get the better of me and I'll unzip the blind and head home to grab a bite to eat. Usually, when this happens, the sound of the zipper startles a herd of deer that had been sneaking up behind me and they race off, bleating in terror. That one simple act will spoil the hunting location for the rest of the year, and I won't see single deer there the rest of the season.

Just poor timing.

On the other hand, I've found that it's impossible to scare deer away from a garden.

I'll slam the front door behind me on my way into work and stomp down the steps, making as much noise as a bull in a china shop. Nine times out of ten, a couple of deer will be just a few dozen yards away, watching me as they placidly chew on my lettuce.

I've even pulled my car to the edge of the garden and honked the horn in an attempt to scare them away. They typically just shoot me an annoyed glance and a look that plainly says, "Try it fat boy. I've got the Game Warden on speed dial and if you so much as lay a finger on me then he'll have your butt *under* the jail."

Deer have very expressive eyes.

Just five months earlier or five months later and I would be able to treat the four-legged destroyers of my property the way the founding fathers intended.

With overwhelming firepower.

As it is, I have to sit back and helplessly watch as they destroy my carefully cultivated garden. Every time I vow to pay them back when deer season rolls around again.

It's all just a matter of timing.

THE SIMPLE GARDEN

◆ ◆ ◆

Gardening is a tradition in the South. Like cornbread, biscuits and gravy, and a deep mistrust of anyone who pronounces their consonants too clearly, it's part of who we are. So ingrained is gardening in our culture, that if you were to tell a southerner that you don't have a garden, they would look at you like you'd just kicked a puppy while wearing a shirt featuring William T. Sherman holding a lit match.

It's who we are.

As is my usual pattern, I started my own garden this year. And as is my usual pattern, I regretted it before I got halfway through tilling.

Aside from the obvious benefits of growing your own food such as fresh air, exercise, and wholly organic produce, gardening also offers you the opportunity of introspection. There's something about turning the dark earth over, smelling the rich organic mixture as it's warmed by the sun, that just naturally leads a person to deep thoughts, allowing the mind to relax and wander as it sees fit.

I myself had several such moments as I worked in my garden. Thoughts like "why did I make it so big, half this size would have been enough" and "why am I doing this, I don't even *like* vegetables. When was the last time I even *ate* a vegetable" and "is it normal for my side to go numb like that?". Usually, these thoughts are had while leaning against the tiller, gasping for breath as sweat trickles into my eyes and blinds me.

You can also make some interesting discoveries while gardening. I discovered early on that, contrary to popular scientific theory, rocks are not formed deep within the earth's mantle by incalculable heat and immense pressure. No indeed, rocks are a winter crop that you get to harvest every spring as you till your garden.

Not to be immodest, but I have had some truly spectacular rock crops in my day.

There's nothing like the reverberating clang that travels through the tiller and up your arm every few feet as you discover another rock. It's enough to bring a tear to your eyes. It often does to me.

It's also fun to interact with nature as you work in the garden. Bugs will invariably wander over to see what the sweating, swearing, fat man is doing and, when that gets boring, they usually decide to take a bite out of you to see how you taste.

They must like it, because they usually come back for more.

At the end, if you work hard all summer and tend to it every day, you will be rewarded with the equivalent of $100 worth of groceries.

And if that doesn't seem worth it to you, well, I guess you just ain't from around here.

AND THEN THERE WERE FUN

◆ ◆ ◆

My motto has always been: "Life's too serious to be taken seriously." At this point, I can't remember if I coined that phrase myself or stole it from somewhere, but it's just silly enough for me to have come up with all by myself.

As silly as the saying is, however, I still hold that it's true. Life can be a brutal, terrifying, and downright scary journey. As one comedian said, "Life's like carrying on a conversation, you're crazy if you try to do it alone." I'm blessed enough to be able to say I've got someone to share my journey with in the form of my sweet, long-suffering wife.

Even with such a stalwart companion beside me, life can still be a challenge. With this in mind, I made a decision many years ago to try to face each day with a tongue in cheek attitude, never taking too seriously anything that I didn't have to take seriously.

It's been recommended that we should all do one good deed a day, a recommendation that I support, but I'll narrow it down and say that we should all do one *funny* thing each day. Take the mundane and turn it into the mirthful. Each one of us will encounter the opportunity to make something funny, we should seize it and enrich the lives of others.

Just think of how much joy the ancient Egyptians could have given modern-day archeologists if they had packed their sarcophagi with confetti cannons. After the initial terror of making their way through a booby-trapped pyramid only to have your ultimate objective explode at the first touch, I imagine the archeologist would have appreciated the injection of levity into their dull, dusty lives.

Now to be clear, I'm not saying I advocate stuffing your pockets with fireworks before you pass away just to liven up the crematorium's day. I'm just saying we should look into the possibility.

All professions have the opportunity to liven people's day up in this way. Grocery store clerks could stick rubber snakes in with the food as they're bagging it up, plumbers could show up to jobs wearing wetsuits. Even doctors, one of the most serious of all professions, could get in on the action, throwing in the occasional 'uh-oh' or 'oops' or even 'what the heck?' in the middle of their examinations.

What I'm trying to say is, we are surrounded by opportunities to lighten and enrich the lives of our fellow man. We are all born with that little spark of insanity, it's our job to nourish and feed it until it grows into a flame which we can all gather round and warm ourselves by.

A FREE RIDE

◆ ◆ ◆

This past Christmas my parents gifted me with something I'd had my eyes on for years. My grandfather's classic truck. Perhaps 'classic' is used more liberally than it should be when words like 'broke-down' or 'rust-heap' work just as well, but to me it was a classic.

The rearview mirror had a tendency to keep falling off, but I discovered if I held the arm in my teeth just right, I could see out the back window, assuming I didn't turn my head.

I also noticed that it was riding a bit rough and figured it might need a new tire or two. Proudly, I drove up to the mechanic and exited in a puff of smoke. He looked it over for about half an hour before giving me the verdict.

The tires had apparently been on since the Reagan administration, which puzzled the mechanic since the car hadn't been manufactured till the Bush administration. Needless to say, they needed replacing. After shelling out only slightly over double the value of the truck, I left with a set of gleaming new tires.

I hadn't yet made it home when a rattling noise began to fill the cab. Employing the tried and true tactic of married men everywhere, I elected to ignore the annoying sound in hopes that it would go away. And just like married men all over the world I learned to my chagrin that the noise had been trying to tell me something.

Namely that my entire muffler had fallen off and was now being drug behind the truck. Thinking quickly, I slammed on the brakes and jumped out of the cab, quickly using some Power Words to lament my situation. (Power Words are those words that dads use around their children, usually when working on projects around the house, when the mother isn't around.)

Luckily, I was only in the middle of a moderately powerful thunderstorm at the time and after a mere half-hour of writhing around in the mud, I was able to get the muffler disentangled and loaded into the bed. I climbed back in and found the missing muffler had added a pleasing roar to the sound of the little truck. Well as much as a 4-cylinder can be said to roar, really more of an enraged squeak than anything else.

"This is fine." I reassured myself, "Why, people pay thousands of dollars to have their trucks sound like this, and I got it for free!" Suitably consoled, I put it in drive and made my slow way home. The windshield wipers didn't work so I had to reach out the window and continuously wipe it clear with my shirt, but you have to make small sacrifices when you drive a classic.

POP-NOTCH

◆ ◆ ◆

Human innovation, and a determined spirit, are a constant source of amazement to me. I'm the sort of man that will never wear a particular item of clothing again if someone mocks it a single time, yet there are individuals that persist in their beliefs despite persecution and a lifetime of ridicule. These are men that have a singular purpose, an indomitable will, and a rock-solid belief in what they are dedicating their life too.

We can find no greater example of this than by the man who invented popcorn.

Little is known about this individual as his name has been lost to the mists of time, but he left the world a creation that will endure to the very end. No one knows what gave him the idea to explode food, or indeed, how many different food items he had to go through before finally settling on corn, but we can assume the list was long.

Mankind as a whole is resistant to change, so when word got around that an enterprising young man was blowing up perfectly good food in the pursuit of a new *kind* of food, we can assume it did not go over well. We can predict he was met with ridicule, scorn, and possibly even violence as he exploded legumes, vegetables, and fruit, all in search of his snack-time holy grail.

Nevertheless, he persisted, and in due time he was rewarded with the fluffy white treat we associate with movie time.

Popcorn is a marvel of modern culinary art; low in calories, filling, and seemingly designed on a molecular level to absorb the greatest of all of mankind's inventions, butter.

It takes a perfectly suitable food, corn, and elevates it to the highest of culinary delights. It's great for snacking, dieting, leisure, and even a meal on the go. Portable and easy to prepare, it's the perfect food for bachelors and the cooking challenged the whole world over.

More than that, it serves as a constant inspiration to us all to follow the inward compass that we all have that constantly seeks to drive us to greatness. It teaches us to disregard the naysayers and those who would seek to discourage us and to pursue that which we have a genuine passion for.

No matter how foolish your idea may seem to others, follow it to the end. So write that book, go back to school, take up painting or invent that doo-dad that you've been thinking about for years. And if there's some food that you imagine would taste better exploded, by all means, blow it up. It worked for popcorn.

WANTED: DEAD OR ALIVE

◆ ◆ ◆

I came home from work the other day to find my wife waiting for me in the living room.

"I saw your poster while I was in town today." She said cheerfully.

"Oh *bleep*." I said as I raced past her. "Just let me explain." I yanked the suitcase from under the bed and hurriedly began filling it with armfuls of clothes. "Just know that the goat was being a jerk, he threw the first punch. I don't even think it was a real petting zoo, the guy had a hook hand and-"

"What are you talking about?" She interrupted me from the doorway.

I stopped, a pair of my red footie pajamas clutched in one hand, "Uh, what are *you* talking about?"

"Your speech for the Friend of Pickens County Library later this month, they started putting up the poster for it today. What was all that other stuff with the goat?"

"Oh, haha." I forced a laugh, "Just another one of my jokes of course. Haha." She eyed me uncertainly for a moment then decided to let it go."

Just as well, the last thing I wanted to do was explain why I got into another fight with a barnyard animal. It took her months to let the 'rabbit' thing go. Rabbits are bullies by the way.

The poster she was referring to actually announced my upcoming speech at the Pickens County Library for the Friends of the

Library. Some poor soul made a mistake somewhere in their system and my name came up as a viable candidate to make a speech. I was quick to jump at the opportunity before they caught their error and realized just who they were reaching out to. Now it's in print and I guess they're stuck with me.

The event in question will be at the local library, thus alcohol will not be served. While I do not personally drink, I've been told people usually require it to enjoy being around me so that may be a tactical error on their part. I will come fully prepared to answer all of your burning Simple Man questions such as "You're not really as stupid as you make yourself out to be in your column are you?" and "You didn't really set your yard on fire trying to kill Yellow Jackets did you?" as well as "You write about your wife a lot, how did you manage to get someone to marry *you*?"

The answers to these are "Yes, yes, and Divine Providence."

Be aware, I have been given no restrictions on what I can discuss and a whole hour in which to discuss it. This is either a genius move by the organizers or incredibly poor planning. Only time will tell.

I hope to see you there.

THE LONGEST YARD

◆ ◆ ◆

I was resting in my new recliner the other day when my editor called me up.

"Kevin!" He barked at me, voice loud even over the tiny speakers on my phone.

I winced, holding it away from my ear, "Hey, good to hear from you. My names Caleb by the way. Remember? Been writing with you for three years now."

"That's what I said," He grumbled, " Hey look, I got a great hook for your next 'Thinkings of a Silly Man' article."

I sighed, but let it go.

"The city is hosting a half K race for Saint Patrick's day, I think you should participate, it would be great exposure."

"Half a K!" I squawked, "That's 500! I can't walk 500 miles, then I would have to walk back and that would be 500 more! Then I'd be the man who walked a thousand miles and I assure you I would fall down at your door-"

"Keith," he interrupted me, "You know how much I love your song references but a half K race means half a kilometer. I can hear you typing in the background so let me save you the trouble, a kilometer is less than a mile."

"The metric system is stupid." I sniffed sulkily.

With a promise that I would consider participating, I hung up the phone. My wife came into the living room later to find me limbering up, dressed head to toe in spandex.

"Oh no, not your superhero phase again." She sighed.

"No, these are my work out clothes, I just haven't used them since we got married. I was 70 pounds lighter then but can you be-lieve they still fit?"

She winced and averted her eyes as I bent over to display their elasticity.

"Please tell me you're not going out wearing that."

"I certainly am, I'm going to be participating in a race." I said proudly, "I'm going to run a whole half K marathon!"

"Isn't that just a little over 1600 feet?" She asked dubiously. "That hardly constitutes a marathon. Our yard is almost that big, and you have trouble walking that without getting winded."

I shrugged, "My editor thinks it will be good exposure."

She eyed the strained spandex as I stretched again, "That's what I'm worried about. Exposure."

"Boy, it will be great to get back into jogging," I said, ignoring her. " I used to do it all the time, I even had my own nickname. They called me Rolling Thunder, on account of the noise my belly used to make as it slapped my thighs."

She rolled her eyes, "I still don't think it's a good idea."

I laughed at her concern, "Nonsense, what's the worst that could happen? Now come help me, I bent at a bad angle and now I can't straighten back up."

DEATH AND TAXES

◆ ◆ ◆

We're rapidly approaching the day of the year that adults in this country dread the most: tax day. Christmas day for the government, April 15th is a time of year when the most powerful government in the world looks at its citizens and tells them to pay up.

On one hand, it's touching that the government has so much faith in us. The same government that feels its citizens are so dumb they have to put warning labels on cigarettes informing us they cause cancer, simultaneously trusts us enough to perform advanced mathematics. They give us a list of bizarre, Byzantium rules about what is taxable, what can be written off, and what we have to pay, then sits back and waits for the money to come rolling in. It's a pretty good racket.

When I was younger, I didn't understand how taxes worked. As I grew older and went to college, however, I came to realize that I *really* didn't understand how taxes work. Still don't as a matter of fact. Basically, the government knows exactly how much you owe them, but they won't tell you, leaving it up to you to figure it out on your own. They hold that information back, then charge you extra money if you make a mistake.

There's an old joke that the government came down so hard on the Mafia only because the government hates competition, but that's an unfair comparison in my opinion.

The Mafia occasionally had mercy on people that owed them money.

There's not just one kind of tax either; there's a tax on how much money you earn, tax on the money you spend, even tax on the money you save. Pretty much anything you interact with or do during your waking hours is taxed or regulated to some extent.

There is currently no tax for things you dream about, but rest assured that the IRS is working on that as we speak.

America has always had a very special relationship with taxation (some of you may remember a certain war fought over it in the late 1700s) and now, almost 300 years later, we can finally say that we have perfected the art of administering taxes imperfectly.

No matter how much we complain about it, taxes are an unavoidable fact of life. The only thing we can do is leave our jobs, go home, and spend our free time calculating how much of our money we owe the government. It's an unpleasant, but necessary, evil.

So tighten up your belt-buckles, grit your teeth, and try not to moan too much when you sign that check over to the IRS.

I'm sure they'll spend it wisely, right?

VICIOUS CIRCLE

◆ ◆ ◆

It is an immutable fact of life that work only leads to more work. The simplest of tasks wind up leading to more tasks until eventually, you wind up in a whirlwind of never-ending chores.

That's why I very seldom do any work around the house.

I experienced this phenomenon in person just a few weeks ago. My wife was wanting to run into town and pick up a few things for the house and asked if I would like to go with her. I said that I would, right after I cranked up my mower to ensure it would run when spring came.

I made my way out to the building where we keep the green behemoth stored, unaware of the heartache I was about to subject myself to. Let me reiterate; this should have been a simple task. Crank the engine, let it idle for a few minutes, and then off to the store. Ten minutes tops.

When I turned the key, however, the mower just coughed a few times and died. The battery was dead.

"No problem," I said with forced cheer as I tried to tamp down on the growing sense of dread I felt. "I'll just pull the truck around and jump it off."

I grabbed the jumper cables and went to move the truck around. When I got to the truck, I found it had a flat tire.

"No big deal," I said, still grinning through gritted teeth. "I'll just bring the air compressor out."

I trudged back to the building and grabbed the air compressor. After lugging it the few hundred yards to the truck, I discovered the cord was too short to reach the outlet, so back to the building

I went for an extension cord. As I unspooled the extension cord, however, I noticed that rats had chewed a hole halfway through it. Muttering curses, I went back inside for some electrical tape.

"When you go back out," my wife said to my backside as I rummaged through the bottom cabinet, looking for tape that I *knew* had to be there somewhere. "Can you take the garbage with you?"

Finally, after the garbage was taken out, the extension cord was repaired, and the tire re-inflated, I was able to jump my mower off.

I sat there on the seat, sweaty and annoyed, but relieved that something else hadn't gone wrong. About that time there was a high-pitched whine and the smell of burnt rubber. I quickly shut the engine off but the damage had been done.

The drive belt had been rubbed in two.

Slowly I climbed off the mower and went inside to tell my wife I wouldn't be able to go with her into town.

There was just too much work to do.

THE GREATEST GIFT

◆ ◆ ◆

Billions of dollars are spent each year in advertising. TV, newspaper, magazines, and billboards all cover us in a deluge of information. Advertising, as any first-year college student will tell you, is all about establishing a need. It seeks to create a problem you didn't know you had, then offer a solution to this new problem. It's a pretty good racket and has led to some of the greatest inventions of the 20th century.

The majority of advertising, recently, has been targeted towards gift ideas. With the Christmas holidays, giant corporations try to tell you that the amount you value your loved ones can be measured by how much you buy for them. Husbands, if you really love your wives, you have to buy them an enormous, shiny rock to wear on a ring. Or you need to buy them a new car, or maybe you should buy them a new exercise bike.

For the record, it is almost never a good idea to buy your wife unsolicited exercise equipment. It will almost certainly be taken the wrong way and then you'll get to experience what sleeping on the couch for a few nights feels like.

The fact remains, it's disgusting and shallow that companies try to tell us the only way to show our love is to go in debt and buy bigger, fancier, shinier items for our loved ones. The truth of the matter is, the absolute best way to show your love for someone, is to just tell them. The best gift we can give our family is to simply spend time with them, making memories that never decay or have to be replaced like the physical items that are being pushed on us.

At least, that's what I always thought. Then my wife got me a recliner for my birthday.

It's cloth, which makes napping a much less sweaty affair than leather couches, and reclines all the way back into the prone position. The footrest is electric so, instead of having to go through all the physical work of reaching down, grabbing a lever, and pulling, I can just press a single button.

It is quite possibly the laziest, most decadent, completely needless gift that has ever been given to me.

It's also my favorite.

To my friends and family, the times we have spent together have been the greatest of my life. They are a treasure that I shall keep and carry with me always.

But those memories don't have a seat warmer, unlike my brand-new recliner. So, if you need me, just call. I'm afraid I won't be leaving the house for quite some time.

TEMPUS FUGIT

◆ ◆ ◆

Time flies. It's a common saying, one that I've heard ever since I was a kid, but the truth of it never really sank in until I began to grow older. As my next birthday draws ever closer, and with it the end of my 20's, I've been thinking of another time related saying.

"Old age is steadily advancing. Towards what, I'm not sure, but I'm fairly certain it's up to no good."

I'll admit, I've been having something of a mortality crisis the past few months. I finally turned to my wife for comfort, certain that she would have words that would calm my silent dread.

"I almost feel like I'm having a midlife crisis," I said jokingly. "Isn't that silly?"

"I don't know about that." She said, idly turning the page of the magazine she was reading. "If you don't start eating better like I've been telling you to, 30 might really be the middle of your life."

No help there. I stomped off into my study, defiantly grabbing a bag of powdered donuts as I went. She came in a few minutes later to find me, covered in white powder as I stared sullenly at the wall. She sat awkwardly on the arm of my chair and patted my shoulder comfortingly.

"I know you're worried about getting older, but nothings going to change." She said, smiling down at me. "You won't even be able to tell a difference. I've never met a man more suited to old age than you are."

I looked up at her hopefully as I brushed crumbs from my beard. "Do you really mean that?"

"Of course I do. What other man in their 20's has as many back problems as you do? Or hates millennials as much as you do? And just the other day I heard you muttering about kids getting off your lawn."

"Well, what's wrong with that?" I muttered, "I didn't want the grass damaged."

"Of course you didn't dear." She patted my hand reassuringly. "And just look at all the benefits of getting older; bluebird specials, being in bed by 8 PM, driving 15 miles under the speed limit. All things that you already love doing."

"Well, when you put it that way..." I said and she continued.

"Walking to the mailbox wearing just your bathrobe, sleeping with your socks on, your love of bingo-"

"Ok, ok I get it," I said, waving her up. "Maybe getting older isn't such a bad thing after all."

I felt better as we made our way back into the living room and settled back into our chairs. Her reading her magazine, me working on my crossword puzzle.

THE BIG CHEAP

◆ ◆ ◆

My wife is the most generous person I know. Her greatest joy is to spend the holiday season shopping for others. She will spend countless hours standing in line, or fighting through jostling crowds just to buy some little gizmo or other that she knows a loved one will enjoy.

Typically, that loved one is me.

When the time comes for her to name something, she wants for herself, the answer is typically a vague "Oh it doesn't matter, anything will do." Or some essential household item. Last year she asked for new towels for the bathroom.

I tried explaining to her that Christmas is for frivolous gifts and not for things that are actually useful, but she paid me no mind.

In contrast to my wife's giving, generous spirit, I am what charitable people would call 'thrifty'. I hate spending money with a passion. I'm the only person I know that watched a Christmas Carol and lauded Scrooge for his sensible wage structure.

In other words, I'm cheap.

Most of the year that doesn't cause any issues. As a rule, I try to interact with people as little as possible, so my miserly nature doesn't come up very often. Around Christmas time, however, it can get a little tricky. This year my wife told me she wanted me to do some of the shopping myself.

"You're always so Grinchy this time of year." She told me, "I want you to understand the true joy of giving."

Privately I thought to myself that I always felt the most joy whenever I socked away money in my 401K or some other interest-bearing account rather than spend it on gifts that would be collecting dust within a month. Of course, I wasn't dumb enough to say that out loud in front of her. Instead, I just smiled and said that I thought it was a good idea.

The next weekend I went shopping for actual Christmas gifts for the first time in years. To my surprise, the gift-buying went rather quickly. I bought items for nearly everyone on my list at the first stop, save one. I couldn't decide between two items, so I finally decided to ask my wife's advice.

"Would your mother like a blue, or pink plastic dinnerware set?" I asked when she picked up the phone.

She hesitated before answering, "Where did you find a pink plastic dinnerware set?"

"At the Dollar store." I said proudly, "I went ahead and picked up your family's Christmas presents here too. Cost me less than 20 bucks for the whole lot!"

There was a long pause on the other end of the line and then she let out a long, slow sigh.

"Put everything back." She said finally, "I'll do the shopping myself."

COMMON SCENTS

◆ ◆ ◆

Recently I was dragged along on another one of my wife's shopping outings. Normally that would mean an afternoon of grocery shopping, but after a recent incident herein I got into an argument with an employee about just how many free samples a person was allowed to take at one time, I have been banned from grocery shopping for the foreseeable future.

Instead, I had to go *girl* shopping with her. Girl shopping is where women go to different stores that all sell the same thing, at the same price. 15,000 different kinds of body washes line the floor, each claiming to do something different, accompanied by 20,000 different shampoos. Why someone needs that many different cleaners is beyond me. I have one bottle that cleans my body and my hair. I even used it to clean my truck once.

The only difference I can spot between the stores are the different types of perfume filling the air. I walked into the first store and nearly fell to the floor so strong was the scent. It was like all the overweight female relatives in the world gathered me up into a hug at the same time, suffocating me in their floral-scented perfume.

"Stop being dramatic." My wife hissed at me as I clawed at my throat. "It's not that bad."

"Are you kidding me?" I choked, "I think this is what police use against riots." She turned and marched me back out of the store before I could finish fashioning my shirt around my face into an improvised gas mask. I waited in the car while she shopped, smug that I had managed to slip out of an afternoon in the suffocating building.

My smugness turned to horror, however, when she came out of the store several hours later, arms laden with bags that smelled like piles of rotting flowers. I found to my dismay, that my wife actually *liked* the cloying scents. Apparently, the perfume that had nearly sent me into an asthmatic shock, was popular.

I resolved right then and there that I was going to design a line of scents that appealed to both sexes and thereby end the tyrannical reign the dead flower lobby holds on the scent industry. I'm still working on funding, but in the not so distant future look for my line of scented candles "Scents of the SimpleMan".

There will be smells such as; frying bacon, sawdust, old book, and frying onions. To those of you that look upon that last scent with skepticism, let me ask you; when was the last time you walked into a kitchen when someone was cooking with an onion, and it didn't smell delicious?

That's what I thought. I'll be a millionaire before the end of the year.

THE GREATEST SECRET

◆ ◆ ◆

Men are designed to be alpha predators; hunter-gatherers with the innate drive to protect our mates and children with our very lives if necessary. We are given to acts of bravado, of reckless abandon, that is incomprehensible to the more sensible gender. The reason behind this is we are driven by our biology to be physical, rather than emotional.

The thought occurs to me that I typed that very macho sounding sentence while wearing fuzzy bunny slippers, eating food my wife picked up and prepared, and gently petting my 5-pound Yorkie, but the general idea is sound.

Men are rough creatures.

This worked out very well for us, and humanity as a whole, for many millennia. Women were satisfied if we protected them from marauding bandits, and if we brought home enough saber-tooth tiger for a good meal. It was a good deal for all involved.

Then Valentine's day was invented, and the expectations changed.

It pains me to say that Valentine's day was invented by a man. Just who this man was, no one really knows. As soon other men found out what he had done, the mess he had gotten us into, he quickly changed his name and moved to another country.

To this day, every man on the planet is still searching for the elusive father of our yearly pain. This is how the Illuminati was formed actually, to find this troublemaker. No luck so far, but we'll get him.

But I digress.

For decades men suffered under the yoke of Valentine's day. We spent weeks upon weeks searching for the appropriate gift for our wives. Most of the time this ended in disaster. It seemed bleak for men everywhere, when one man, a shining beacon of hope, invented the gift card. Every time men gather we offer a solemn salute to this mysterious man who has saved us all so much grief and pain.

The gift card is the perfect weapon in a man's simple arsenal. To a man, the greatest gift you can give someone is money. It confused us, therefore, when it became socially unacceptable to give as a 'thoughtful' gift. So, the compromise was made that we would place the money on a small plastic card with colorful graphics. Luckily the women accepted this and peace was restored.

The gift-buying mentality of a man can be summed up thusly; I like you this much amount of money but I'm not really sure what you like. Here's the money (on a card), you do all the work of actually buying your own present.

It remains the greatest scam ever perpetrated in the history of the human race.

Don't tell anyone though, it's a secret.

GOING VIRAL

◆ ◆ ◆

The virus currently sweeping the country is no joke and should be taken seriously. Everyone is taking all necessary precautions to limit exposure and lessen their chances of catching anything

On a personal note, I've recently had a battle with a bad bout of bronchitis coupled with an upper respiratory infection. I was afraid I would only be one ill-timed cough away from getting shot.

Suffice to say, I was not very warmly received when I returned to work from my two-day bout with my cold. I shuffled in the door, bleary-eyed and coughing, and was met with a considerable degree of hostility.

My supervisor, who normally has an open-door policy, kept her door firmly locked all day long. Every time I would glance up I would see her standing in her window, eying me warily. I found friends who I have known for years, who used to welcome my visiting their desk for some idle chatter, suddenly had no time for me.

For weeks, I walked the halls of my office, shunned and ostracized. I found that a single cough, or sniffle, could clear a room out faster than pulling a fire alarm. I'll admit, I grew drunk with my own power. Any time I was asked to sit in on another pointless meeting, I would sniffle pathetically, hack dryly into one hand, and slowly pull myself out of my chair.

"Yeah, I suppose I could sit in." I would say thickly. I was quickly excused from having to participate.

One day a coworker brought in a box of donuts. I spied a group of people gathered excitedly around and figured I would check it out. The crowd quickly parted as I approached. I shuffled up to the desk, leaned over, and took a big whiff. "Boy these smell good," I said, throwing in a little wheeze for effect. "Can I have two?"

"Just take the whole box." My coworker said as she quickly backed up, the crowd had already disappeared. "Please, I insist."

I'm not proud of it, but with a little cough, and a little sneeze, a man can get away with just about anything these days.

Be warned though, most people in this county are armed. You may find that it could be hazardous to your health getting sick these days.

WHO WAS THAT UN-MASKED MAN?

◆ ◆ ◆

I left my home for the first time in weeks just the other day. Like the groundhog, I emerged from my den, blinking, and dazzled by the strange, shining object in the sky. I saw my shadow and ran back inside, foretelling six more weeks of quarantine. Once I summoned my courage to leave my property, I found a world straight out of a Hollywood movie.

Restaurants were closed, stores were mandating masks. Even the traffic was almost nonexistent. The drivers that were on the road drove like they were extras from Mad Max, weaving and zipping in and out of the more sane vehicles. My sleepy little town had transformed into an apocalyptic wasteland.

Somehow, I was able to make it to my destination without being run down by fellow Jasperites, some of whom seem to believe a jacked-up truck means they have to drive inches from the car in front of them.

Now, first of all, let me say that I wholeheartedly advocate wearing a mask. Doctors have worn them for decades and I don't feel like my rights are being infringed if I'm asked to put one on. That being said, this particular day I wasn't wearing one.

I could give you a lot of reasons; I just thought I was dropping my car off and wouldn't interact with people, I thought I would be in and out. But the simple truth of the matter is, I simply forgot. As soon as I walked into the lobby, there were gasps from the customers inside. Eyes narrowed over their narrow strips of cloth as they watched me approach the cashier.

By the time I reached the desk, I was bowed nearly double with the accumulated rage and condemnation of a lobby full of people. The cashier stared at me as their eyes, the only part of their face visible, widened with shock. She (I assume it was a she, but these days I'm just not sure) leaned slightly away from me as I handed my keys over. She reached one gloved hand out and gingerly took them off the counter, careful not to touch any more than she absolutely had to.

I meekly made my way to a corner and sat, my head bowed. Every eye in the room was on me as we all waited. You could feel the tension ramping up, and I heard them begin muttering to themselves, noise muted by their masks. Finally, I couldn't take it anymore. I stood up and walked outside as quickly as I could. A muted cheer went up from the crowd as I left.

It was almost loud enough to drown out the sound of a lock being turned into place behind me.

Almost.

HELLO WALLS

◆ ◆ ◆

For those of you who might not be aware, strange things are afoot in the world. Travel is restricted, gatherings are outlawed, and, a true sign of the apocalypse, the government has moved back tax day.

You know things are bad if Uncle Sam is saying it's ok to miss a payment.

When quarantine orders first came down from the highest levels of government, I quickly read through them, eager to do my civic duty and limit the spread. I soon found out, much to my surprise, that I had been doing my civic duty for years without even knowing about it.

The orders said to stay home and unless absolutely necessary: not a problem. Additionally, it said to limit contact with others; done and done. Finally, it said to avoid going to the grocery store if possible.

I haven't gone to the grocery store since I got married. I couldn't even tell you where the nearest grocery store was.

My biggest takeaway from the orders was that I know had an excuse, in writing, from the President of the United States, saying I didn't have to go to any family gatherings.

It was a dream come true. Birthdays, weddings, social gatherings, Sunday dinners, I was able to skip them all with impunity. It was just like before I got married and gained a conscience in the form of a fiery little redhead.

Most days I spend snacking and napping, which isn't too much of a change from my pre-quarantine life. The only difference is how much more of it I'm able to do now.

The biggest loser in my home is my wife. Not only is she stuck at home for the foreseeable future, but she's also stuck at home with *me.*

No amount of writing can accurately convey what she has to go through so I'll just give you a minute to let your own imagination conjure the horrors.

Still with us? Good.

All in all, she's been a good sport about the whole matter. The woman has the patience of a saint and a heart the size of the moon. Just last night I awoke to find her tucking me in, her kind, loving hands pressing my cover down around my neck to make sure I didn't catch a chill.

So sweet was the gesture, I almost hated to stop her, but eventually, the covers got so tight it began to cut off my air and I had to ask her to stop. She seemed disappointed but I overheard her muttering something about getting me the next night.

That's just the kind of woman she is, kind to a fault.

DEATH OF A SIMPLE MAN

◆ ◆ ◆

I do stupid things, rapidly and often. While it makes for great columns, it does wreak havoc on my health insurance premiums. Most people are pretty happy with the way I live my life. My editor is pleased with my shenanigans, they make for good reading, and the readers seem to enjoy them. But it's not the safest way to make it through life. Some of my antics have gotten so dangerous that I've heard that funeral directors look for my weekly column, only to turn away, disappointed when there's not an obituary featured.

One day, after I turned in a column detailing a particularly dangerous adventure (maybe it was the time I tried to rewire my fuse box while standing in ankle-high water, the result of a failed plumbing repair) my editor reached out to me.

"Kyle," he barked when I answered the phone. "I need your obituary."

I was surprised. Obituaries were for dead people. As far as I knew I was still among the living. I had a brief existential crisis as the ending of The Sixth Sense flashed through my memory. But my wife could still see me, had just gotten through yelling at me for spraying weed killer on her begonias as a matter of fact, so I knew I must be alive.

"Why do you need my obituary? If it's about that joke I made about you last week-"

"What joke?" He growled. "You know I don't read your article."

"Oh, uh. Never mind. Obituary?"

"People like you, Kevin. Don't ask me why, I don't see the appeal. When something happens to you, I want to be able to run with it."

"How am I supposed to know how I'm going to die?"

"You're a smart guy, Keith. An idiot, but smart. Figure it out."

Then he hung up. I thought a lot about what he said, and finally sat down and typed up an obituary. None of us know how we're going to die, but history teaches me it will probably be as a result of something stupid I've done, so I created a MadLibs style, fill in the blanks obituary. He can do the rest of the work.

Caleb Smith, local writer, passed not so peacefully today at his home while repairing a ______. He was surrounded by loved ones, his two dogs, and first responders, who have his address memorized. Authorities say the (smoke/explosion/electrical discharge) were seen for miles around. When pressed for comment about his timely demise, officials only had this to say.

"While tragic, Mr. Smith's death was completely avoidable. We urge the community to use common sense when performing household repairs. Please make sure you are not covered in (gas/water/angry yellow jackets) when working on (electrical circuits/the roof/running equipment)."

The Pickens Progress will miss Mr. Smith. Auditions for his replacement will commence this Thursday. All applicants must be able to spell their name, this is the extent of the requirements.

CATCH 22

◆ ◆ ◆

This article is typically a place for levity and humor. It has become, I hope, a refuge for people from the seriousness of a world that's slowly sinking further and further into madness. Today, however, I would like to talk about something serious. A subject that has affected me personally, as well as millions of Americans. Obesity.

Obesity is an epidemic in America with recent studies showing that nearly 40% of Americans are considered obese. Congress got involved, issuing calls for food companies to take action. The food companies responded by offering their snacks in smaller, healthier sizes. You'd think they would know better. I'm fat, I don't want less, I want more.

If you really want to create a 'fun size' Snickers bar, make it as long as my arm. That would be fun.

Not too long ago I started noticing packaging in grocery stores claiming, "half the calories!". Initially, I was delighted. This meant that I got to eat twice as much. I quickly scooped up an armful and ran to catch up with my wife. When I got home, however, I was disappointed to discover that 'half the calories' also meant 'half the taste'.

I'm not certain what calories are exactly, but judging from the foods I've tried that are low in them, calories are what gives food its flavor.

Portion control is a big buzzword these days. 'Portion control' means you eat just enough where you're only *slightly* hungry, not ravenous. If you finish a meal and you're actually full, then you've eaten too much. I mentioned this in passing to my grandfather the other day and he laughed.

"That ain't nothing new. We did that all the time when we was kids."

I was surprised, "You practiced portion control when you were a child?"

"Yep," he nodded as he sipped gravy from a coffee mug, "Only we didn't call it portion control back then, we called it the Great Depression. Healthiest I've ever been in my life."

As we sat there, eating our sausage and donut biscuits (a sausage patty sandwiched between two glazed donuts), we discussed the merits of portion control.

"The way I see it." He said as I refilled his mug with the gravy bowl, "Is it's all about moderation. It's ok to eat as much as you want sometimes, but you gotta balance it out with hard work and healthy food too."

I groaned, "Hard work? Isn't there another way?"

Maybe he's on to something though, he's 80 this January and still chops his own firewood. Maybe we just need to pick and choose our vices; should we have a donut, or should we take a nap?

I think, today, I might just do both.

PUPPY LOVE

◆ ◆ ◆

There is no greater feeling in the world than to have a dog choose you over your spouse. A few years back we bought a Yorkie to keep my wife company as she worked on schoolwork. As a lover of all animals, not just the fried kind, I was excited to have a new addition to our home. As we drove the dog home I imagined all the fun we would have. The rainy days where she could curl up in my lap and we could nap together while my wife worked away.

The reality turned out far different.

From the moment we brought the dog home, she had an instant and deep fascination with my wife. Every time she would get up to go to the kitchen or into the other room, our dog would jump to her feet and trot after her, following right at her heels wherever she went.

She would have nothing to do with me.

I would flop into my chair, ready for a nap, and pat my lap and call her name. She would turn one eye to me, staring at me incredulously before giving a dismissive little huff and turning back to gaze lovingly up at my wife. No matter how many treats, toys, or belly rubs I offered, she would always choose my wife over me.

"Nonsense." My wife would say anytime I complained about it. "She loves you just as much as she does me."

And so the next few years passed, Sandy a constant companion for my wife and me with no one to nap with.

Then along came Toby.

Toby is a little Yorkie male that we picked up on Halloween. He is long, lanky, awkward, and has a pair of ears that look like something off a monster costume.

He is also hopelessly attached to me. Where Sandy would follow my wife around the house, Toby would frantically scratch at the door whenever I would leave for work. Where Sandy would stare up from the floor at my wife in adoration, Toby will climb onto my chest just to get closer to me.

In short, I'm his favorite. My wife tells me that he'll sit in her lap when I'm gone, but the second I walk back through our front door, he's trying to get in my lap.

"He hates me." My wife wailed one weekend after failing to get him to leave my lap to play with her. " He only cares about you!"

"Nonsense." I quoted back to her as I slowly and smugly petted the dog in my lap, "He loves you just as much as he loves me."

It was a lie of course. I'm his favorite, and it's a grand feeling.

SNOW WAY OUT

◆ ◆ ◆

Multiple weather sources have now listed their winter forecasts for the upcoming season, and I'm afraid to say it's not looking too good for North Georgia. The weatherman has given us equal chances for above or below-average precipitation as well as above average or below-average temperatures.

This means we are likely to have a lot of snow this winter, or maybe none at all. Temperatures are either going to be frigid, or balmy and sunny. Given the wonders of modern meteorology, we are blessed to have such ample warning so far in advance, so the time to prepare is now, don't wait until it's too late.

To get ready for the upcoming temperatures, everyone reading this needs to make sure they have an ample supply of firewood or a window unit air conditioner. Also, make sure that everyone in your household has a warm winter coat, or at the very least a comfortable pair of shorts.

With the projected chances of snow, people need to be sure that they have snow chains ready for their vehicles, or just leave the tires as they are. Snowy roads can be deadly and warm roads can be quite safe to drive on. Please be sure that you're taking the appropriate precautions as we go through the treacherous and/or quite pleasant winter months.

It is essential that you have at least a two-week supply of food and clean water in case of the equally likely and unlikely event of a winter storm. If for any reason you cannot put in a supply of food in time, you can always go out and enjoy one of the many fine eateries Jasper has to offer. The roads will be quite safe to drive on. Or maybe they won't.

If you have children in your house, you will need to stock up on activities to keep them occupied during long stretches of the type of weather we're expected to have. Board games are a great choice, considering the type of winter they're calling for, or maybe a slip-n-slide or perhaps a badminton set. Pretty much anything that will keep their minds occupied for long periods of time without power, or summer-like temperatures.

It's also highly recommended you invest in a sled or set of fishing poles before winter begins in earnest. Outdoor activities can be so enjoyable during the winter and you don't want to miss out on all the fun a winter wonderland/prime fishing weather day has to offer.

Again, we should all be thankful to have received such important information so early in the season so we can all adequately prepare for what may, or may not, be coming.

MIDNIGHT RUN

◆ ◆ ◆

Every night for the past few years, like clockwork, I will wake up at 2 A.M. with an insatiable hunger for sweets. What this means is that every night for the past few years I have had to wage a war between my own desires, and my will power. So of course, I have had sweets every night for going on three years now.

The first time this happened my wife shuffled into the kitchen to find me standing over the sink with my eyes closed, eating a slice of cheesecake with my bare hands.

"Darn it, he's sleepwalking." She muttered to herself.

"Sleepwalki-? Oh, right, uh I mean. Zzzzz. Oh, I'm so asleep right now."

It didn't take her long to catch on to the fact that I was wide awake and fully aware of what I was doing, despite my rather convincing fake snore.

I've tried everything I could think of to keep from eating sweets in the middle of the night, even taking the drastic action of asking my wife to stop buying sweets altogether.

But my wife, either out of a deep and abiding love for me and the wish to see me happy, or out of a desire to get my life insurance policy, continued to buy sweets in bulk.

I'm not sure what causes such a drive for candy at such an odd hour. I even asked my doctor about it once, hoping he would have some advice about how to cut down on my cravings and stop such an unhealthy practice.

He listened to me patiently as I explained my situation, how I was eating literal fistfuls of candy every night, then calmly and kindly gave me the best medical advice I've ever received.

He waited till I was done, then he laid one hand on my knee, looked me straight in the eyes and firmly said, "Don't do that."

He didn't say 'fatty', but it was certainly implied.

So far this hasn't had a noticeable effect on my health, I've weighed roughly the same for the past ten years, and my recent lab work was what one doctor begrudgingly called 'good genes in action'. Still, as I get older I can't help but feel that eating thousands of calories at 2 A.M. may not be entirely healthy. Call it a feeling I get sometimes, usually in the left side of my chest after expending the slightest amount of effort.

I should probably try a little harder to resist the urge, but there's something about a pack of Nutter Butters and a cold glass of milk at 2 A.M. that just really hits the spot.

THE GOOD HUSBAND

◆ ◆ ◆

I'm not the best husband in the world. I'm loud, messy, and have dining habits that would embarrass a sow. In addition to that, I have an unsettling tendency to set my wife's prized plants on fire. My wife, by contrast, is an angel. No matter how hard her day is, no matter how busy, she unfailingly has dinner prepared, the house cleaned, and my clothes for the next day washed and ironed.

One day I only worked a half-day, so in a fit a husbandly motivation, I decided to try to return the favor. I walked into the laundry room, grabbed an armful of clothes, packed the washer to the brim, and turned it on. I didn't remember the washer rocking so roughly from side to side when she did laundry, but to be fair I never paid much attention.

Next, I went to wash the dishes. That went easily enough, although after I had loaded the washer up, I discovered that I couldn't find the dish detergent. Shrugging, I retrieved the laundry detergent and filled the little basin with that, figuring one soap would work just as well as the next.

Feeling accomplished, I decided to make dinner. Since my culinary repertoire is limited, I decided on the safe option of bacon. I like bacon. It's a good honest food. Even though medical professionals have all reached a consensus that bacon is actively trying to kill you, it's still a favorite of mine.

Bacon is the only food that tries to warn you before you eat it. The burning hot grease popping onto your skin is bacons way of saying, "If I hurt you this much just preparing me, imagine what

I'm doing to your arteries."

I like to know where I stand with my food.

I turned the music on to cover up the increasingly alarming sounds the washing machine was making, and just got in the groove of cooking. Happy that I was doing something for my wife for a change. So engrossed was I in my good deed, I didn't notice the pool of suds pouring from the dishwasher until I stepped in it.

The plate of bacon went flying as I executed a perfect 3-point spin. Had I been in the Olympics I'm certain I would have won bronze, if not silver, for that little bit of acrobatic finesse, if I had only stuck the landing. My wife walked in the door just then to find me laying in a pool of soap. The washing machine was now screaming as it did it's best to rock the house off its foundation.

She stared at me, shocked. I smiled and opened my mouth to offer an explanation, just as a slice of bacon fell from where it had stuck to the ceiling, landing on my upturned face. With a heavy sigh, she took off her coat and went to work.

HOME SWEET HOME

◆ ◆ ◆

My wife has an annoying tendency of wanting to go out and do things. No matter how often I explain to her that I work very hard to pay for our house and that we should enjoy the fruits of my labor, it continues to fall on deaf ears. She likes to go to new places, meet new people, and have new experiences. To behold the majesty of the world around us as she takes fresh delight in each new thing.

Personally, I prefer my familiar old recliner. I've just gotten to the point where there's a Caleb shaped imprint in it. You just can't pay for that level of comfort.

Just the other day she came into the house to find me perfecting my imprint, "You hungry?" She asked.

"Almost perpetually, what's for supper?"

"Well, there's this new restaurant in town I thought we could try." And off we went again. I tried to explain to her that we had perfectly good food in the house, but she replied food was more enjoyable when you didn't have to cook it for yourself. Since I hadn't cooked for myself in almost six years, I couldn't argue with her logic. So I sighed, tucked my belly back into my shirt, and put my shoes on to leave.

That's another downside of constantly going out and doing things; you have to look all presentable for people. Home is where you can let your belly flop out, free from judgment. Well, home and Wal-Mart I suppose, but I prefer my home.

There's just a level of comfort to be found at home. You can wear what you want, say what you want, and eat as much as you want. Certain Italian based restaurants may claim to have all you can eat breadsticks, but after you ask for the sixth or seventh basket, managers start getting involved.

That never happens at home.

Another benefit of being at home is that you can fall asleep whenever, and wherever you want. If I'm watching a movie and I drift off to sleep, I know I'll wake up in the same spot, safe and sound. You fall asleep in a movie theater and the next thing you know a drifter sitting next to you has braided your beard hair while your wife is engrossed in the movie.

To be fair that's only happened twice so far.

I suppose it says a lot about me as a person that, when I watch Police shows, I always feel a certain amount of envy for the perp who's sentenced to house arrest.

Six months where I can't leave the house? Where do I sign up?

THE GREAT FATSBY

◆ ◆ ◆

I shuffled into the living room the other day, holding up a pair of my pants, "Honey, I think you shrunk my clothes in the wash." I said.

My wife's head whipped up, eyes narrowing at the implied criticism of her housekeeping, "I did no such thing." She said tartly, "Put them on, let me see."

Sighing, I pulled my pants on, straining as I tried to close the clasp, "See? They've definitely shrunk."

She got up from the table and walked over, reaching down to pat my stomach, "I don't think they've shrunk, I think you've grown. You're getting a little tummy on you." I protested that I hadn't but she wouldn't hear it. She marched me into the bathroom and made me stand on the scale to prove once and for all if it was her washing or her cooking that was to blame for my tight pants.

The flashing, digital numbers on the scale proved that her washing was fine.

"Well, it looks like you're just going to have to go on a diet." She said.

"A diet?", I wailed.

"Well, it's either that or buy new clothes."

"Spend money?" I wailed even louder.

Eventually, my love of money outweighed my love of food, so we settled on the diet. We sat down that night and worked out a diet plan together. My initial enthusiasm died down when she began to cross off all the foods that I loved and held dear. No more sweets, no more chips, no more greasy, salty, fried food. I even shed a tear when she firmly informed me that 'taco salad' doesn't count as an actual salad and was therefore off the menu.

She wasn't even consistent with her rules. First, she told me I needed to eat more greens, then in quick succession, she marked out skittles, M&Ms, and sour tarts. Totally blind to the fact that all of those snacks were packed with greens.

I left the table a broken man, filled with shattered dreams. My heart was so heavy when I left, I'm sure I gained 10 pounds from that alone. We stuck with the diet for almost a month before she finally caved and let me start binging on my favorite foods again. My wife lost a lot of patience in that time, but that's about all that was lost. My pants remained just as tight as ever.

At the end of the month, she took me shopping for new clothes. I trailed along behind her, happily munching on the donuts I held in each hand. Sometimes the least costly avenue is to just spend the money.

WHAT'S IN A NAME?

◆ ◆ ◆

"A rose by any other name would smell as sweet." That was written over 400 years ago by a pretty smart English fella. Now, as an American, I haven't had to care what the British have had to say since 1776, but they still had some good phrases. Best as I can tell, that sentence means that what you call something doesn't matter, because it doesn't change what the thing is.

On one hand, I agree, you can call me a dog all you want (and many people do), but that still doesn't make me a dog. But what you call things does matter, we have entire industries dedicated to coming up with attractive sounding names in order to sell things, and it works. I wouldn't want to eat a "cockroach of the sea boiled with seeds", but "shrimp gumbo" sounds warm and tasty.

That got me to thinking about where we got the words we use in day to day life, specifically, the rooms of our homes. How did that come about? Was there one guy assigned to walk through the first house, naming everything inside for future generations to use?

If so, he should have been fired.

He started out doing a good job. He stepped onto the landing in front of the house and decided that it would be called a "porch", so far so good. He walked in and called that room the "foyer". He went through and came up with such names as the "kitchen", "basement", "attic", and "closet". All thoughtfully and carefully thought up.

Then he started getting lazy. He looked into the room where they kept the beds and decided "bedroom" was a good choice.

Walking into the room where baths were taken, he chose "bathroom." But the one that infuriates me the most, the laziest name of all, is the one I assume he chose as he was leaving.

I can only imagine he was rushing to finish up, in a hurry to get to his next job, or maybe he just had a date that night. He passed by the place where the fire went, looked at it, and jotted down the first thing that came to mind. "Fireplace"

Pure laziness.

I've said it for years, words matter. They change how we perceive the world around us, serve to influence and inspire the human race to new heights. If you don't believe me, look at a comparison I found online:

"If someone invites you to their cottage in the forest, that sounds warm and cozy. If someone invites you to a cabin in the woods, you're going to die."

I THINK NOT

◆ ◆ ◆

Some men have the rare and glorious ability to think of nothing. To clear our mind completely and utterly of anything resembling conscious thought. To quietly, peacefully, live in the moment.

We've created entire sports dedicated to this. Hunting is just men spending thousands of dollars on equipment and gear in order to sit in the woods and think of nothing for hours on end. Fishing is the same thing with an added water feature.

I'm not immune to this phenomenon either; many times I'll go most of an entire day without having anything close to a coherent thought. When I explained this to my wife, she was quick to agree that I was abnormally gifted in this area.

Not everyone understands this gift, however. I can't tell you how many times someone has screamed at me "What were you thinking?" and had to try to explain to them that I was not, in fact, thinking at all.

Life can be hard for the un-thinking gifted.

There are also inherent dangers associated with this, however. I've been sitting alone on a bench at the mall, quietly waiting for my wife to finish shopping, and allowed myself to think of nothing. So complete was my lack of thought, I soon had a crowd of people gathered around me, concerned for my health. Apparently, my vacant, slack expression gave the impression that I was having some sort of mental episode, possibly a stroke.

The key, I've found, is to adopt a pensive look on your face when you're thinking of nothing. A furrowed brow and squinted eyes make for a marvelous mask when you're thinking of nothing. For those suitably advanced, a pipe is an excellent addition to the costume.

I should mention, however, that at no point should the pipe ever be lit. Holding a lit pipe in your teeth while thinking of nothing is a recipe for disaster, especially for those of us with beards. Nothing brings you back down to earth quite like a fire extinguisher to the face while you're trying to think of nothing.

In my defense, the person with the extinguisher overreacted. I would have realized what was happening before my beard moved from a smolder to a full-blown blaze.

Probably.

So ladies, don't worry so much about what your man is thinking of the next time he seems unusually quiet and pensive. If he's staring into the distance, eye unfocused, brow furrowed, chances are he's not thinking of anything at all. And if he takes out his pipe and lights it, leave him alone, no need to run for that fire extinguisher just yet.

Unless you're just looking for an excuse to empty it into your husband's face. My wife was quick to jump at the opportunity.

PAR FOR THE COURSE

◆ ◆ ◆

Golf is a game of precision, requiring pure, unfettered concentration and mental clarity. As such you can imagine my wife's incredulity when I told her I was going to go play a round with some buddies of mine.

The man I was playing with claimed he was only an occasional golfer and wasn't really very good. He was, apparently, a very good liar, however. He teed off and I watched the tiny ball soar hundreds of yards through the air to land a few feet to the left of the little flag.

"Ah shoot." He said, slapping his knee. "I was trying to land it to the right of the flag. Oh well, you see I'm not very good."

Nervously I took my place and swung the club, digging a trench in the green that was so big I later learned they had to turn it into a water hazard. Steadying myself again, I swung once more. This time I missed the ball entirely. Amidst gales of laughter, I teed up again and swung a third and final time. The head of the club struck the ball with a sharp crack, sending it arching across the fairway. I watched in satisfaction as it flew straight. Then, after going about a hundred yards, the ball abruptly veered to the side. It crashed into a tree amidst a puff of brown fur.

"What was that?" I asked my guide, who had been watching the balls progress through his binoculars.

"Uh," he said before lowering the glasses and giving me a wide-eyed stare. "That was a squirrel. You just exploded a squirrel with your golf-ball." For the record, that's more squirrels than I usually bag all season. The next time I go golfing I may slide my rifle in the bag, just in case a buck ambles onto the course.

Then again, my golf clubs were already proving to be more deadly than most of my guns.

The rest of the course went much the same way. We crawled our way through all 18 holes, leaving a trail of divots, broken clubs, and traumatized wildlife in our wake. What had begun as a bright, clear day, soon transformed into a wet, dreary mess. Storm clouds rolled in and we played the last 9 holes in a torrential downpour.

Finally, we arrived at the 18th hole. It was by the parking lot and patrons of the club (who had been watching my antics with glee up to this point) quickly came outside to stand in front of their cars and glare darkly at me. I elected to sit the final hole out.

The next time the man invited me to play I turned him down. Golf is just too stressful.

PATTERNS OF BEHAVIOR

◆ ◆ ◆

We all have certain patterns we adhere to. A certain way we drive to work, a specific day of the week we go to the grocery store, maybe a particular order in which we get ready in the morning. We all have a routine we get in to. Generally, this is a good thing, the subconscious mind takes over and does things automatically, freeing up our conscious mind to think about other things, like what we're having for supper or the love life of certain celebrities. You know, important things.

But sometimes it can be dangerous. The brain goes on auto-pilot and before you know, it's gone and got you in trouble. This happened to me just the other day, conscious brain Caleb checked out, and subconscious Caleb took the wheel and drove my proverbial car right into the ditch.

I'm not proud to admit it, but I've been known to "zone out" when my wife is talking. I believe any man, if he's being honest, would admit to the same thing. I learned a long time ago not to just ignore her, but by listening to the tone and pitch of what she's saying, my brain learned when to interject a "hmmm" or a "that's crazy" and sometimes a "yeah it sounds like it" whenever she pauses in her stories.

For years this served me well, until a few weeks ago. I was sitting in my recliner reading a book and she was sitting on the couch, telling me about how her day had been. It started out with "Janet being a real jerk today", and that's the last thing I heard. I checked out and kept reading my book, and subconscious Caleb kept up the conversation for me. He heard all the little pauses that indicated it was my turn to say something, and provided the needed "mmm, that sounds terrible" and "I can't believe she said that". Everything when ok until she asked a question and I said, "Yeah it sounds like it." I immediately knew I had said something wrong as ice began forming on the pages of my book.

I looked up, wary, to find her staring at me wide-eyed. "Do you really think so?" she asked. Having no idea what had been said, I chose what I assumed was a safe response. "Well sure I do, if that's what you think!" She got up and stormed out of the room.

It took a lot of groveling on my part, and some fancy footwork, to get back in her good graces. It wasn't until a few weeks later I learned what she had even asked me.

"I don't know, do you think I'm just being an idiot?"

A LESSON IN WRITING

◆ ◆ ◆

Recently, a number of people have asked me how I have a new column in the paper every week. I typically just shrug and tell them that it's just part of being a writer. The formulae for being a comedy writer is not a very lengthy one, especially if you don't worry too much about being a particularly funny comedy writer. Extremely funny writers have a much longer process, but this is a burden I don't happen to bear. My formulae can be summed up thusly:

Step 1: Do stupid things.

Step 2: Get hurt in the process.

Step 3: Write an unexaggerated account of what happened.

That's pretty much it. Most people omit the second step, which is their prerogative. Personally, I feel like it adds a certain flair to the story that the first and third steps alone can't quite match.

This is, of course, a simplified list. The actual "process" of writing an article is usually much more in-depth. You have to worry about sentence structure, adjective use, and whether the story is too graphic for a family audience. There are also deadlines you have to worry about. Mine is bright and early, Monday morning. I like to wait till Sunday evening before I even begin to think about what I'm going to write about. The panic of realizing you have nothing to submit in 12 short hours, really kicks off the creative juices. Or at least that's the excuse I use when my wife asks me "Why I put it off until the last minute again."

The real reason is I usually just forget until the last minute. Nothing ruins your night quite like going to bed, then remembering, just as your drifting off to sleep, that you don't have an article to turn in. Wives are not very understanding when you suddenly leap from the bed at midnight, grab your computer, and rush into your study. Especially when your computer is a desk-top, and thus connected to the wall.

Then I have to rack my brain for the dumbest, most family-friendly escapade I have recently gotten myself into. This can take hours.

Finally, it's time to write. As you can see, the actual process of writing taking up a very small portion of delivering an article. This only takes about 30 minutes. Then I have to proofread (my editor will be shocked to learn that the hodge-podge of mis-spelled words and improper grammar he receives each weekend is actually my "proof-read" version) and email it in.

Then I slink off to bed, careful not to wake my wife. Secure in the knowledge that I won't have to worry about writing another article until the next Sunday night.

THE PROPER AMBIENCE

◆ ◆ ◆

As I sit in my study (also called the laundry room) looking out over my frost kissed back yard, I can't help but feel a twinge of regret at the absence of a fireplace in our home. Nothing beats sitting in front of a roaring fire, listening to the howling winter wind as it vainly tries to worm its hoary fingers into hidden cracks in the siding. I picture myself sprawled out in an overstuffed recliner, socked feet stretched out to the warm, crackling flames as rain beats against the window panes.

It's a snug, warm, mental image, infinitely conducive to getting a writer in the proper mindset. Instead, I'm stuck with central heat. A cold, soulless pad lets me set the exact temperature I want the house to be, and a warm breeze wafts up from metal slats in the floor. It's horrible.

Honestly, it's a wonder I was ever able to write a word in conditions like these. A writer needs ambiance, the appropriate setting, in order to be able to write well. No one would have read Hemmingway if he had written The Old Man and the Sea in his laundry room, using his wife's ironing board as a computer desk.

I tried explaining this to my wife once but it fell on deaf ears.

"Writing is about what's up here," she said tapping her temple. "And what's in here." She said, patting her heart.

Which just goes to show she knows absolutely nothing about writing.

Even when we were building the house, she steadfastly refused to let me have a fireplace put in. Something about the thought of me deliberately setting an open flame indoors made her eye start twitching. Personally, I blame it on too much coffee, but I keep those thoughts to myself.

I tried to explain to her that was quite responsible enough to kindle a fire in my own home without burning the whole building down around our ears. She just stared at me stone-faced, eye twitching. Knowing how much she loves a bargain, I tried a different tact.

"Gas is so expensive now," I said. "Look at all the pine trees around the house. We would be set for fuel for years!"

"I thought you weren't supposed to burn pine in a fireplace." She said suspiciously. "Doesn't it set your chimney on fire?"

"Listen to how silly you're being right now." I'd chuckled. "It's a fireplace, there's supposed to be fire in the chimney. That's how it works."

I almost had her convinced until I mentioned how easy it would be to start a fire on cold winters mornings, just a dash of gasoline on the logs and away we go. But then her eye started twitching again and I decided I'd better drop it.

PLAYING POSSUM

◆ ◆ ◆

I've only been in a few wrecks in my life, none of them very serious. I wasn't at fault at any of them either; one, the driver ran a stop sign, one was a young driver making an improper turn, and one was a possum.

Let me explain. Several years ago, I had a bad habit of leaving trash on the porch overnight. The local possum population took this as an open dinner invitation. I would step out the door the next morning and find garbage spread out over half the yard. Instead of doing the mature, responsible thing of just taking the trash all the way to the garbage can, I decided the real problem was the possums.

In the middle of the night, I would wrench the door open, flashlight in hand, hoping to catch the culprits in the act, but they were always too sneaky for me. Until the night of the wreck. This particular night, about midnight, I jerked the door open and caught the fuzzy little miscreant right in the act. With a shout of victory, I raced out onto the porch to chase him off. Unfortunately, he was already well into his act of vandalism when I caught him and trash was already spread across the porch. My bare feet slipped on a pile of used coffee grounds and I fell. Right onto the possum.

Thinking fast, I quickly scrambled off him but it was too late, the possum lay on the porch, dead as a hammer.

My wife came to the door in her nightgown, "What was that high pitched scream?" She asked blearily, "It sounded like a frightened little girl."

"Uh, nothing." I mumbled, "Look, I got the possum."

"Oh, that poor thing." She cried, "Is he dead?"

I quickly explained what happened and confirmed that it was, in fact, dead. "Are you sure?", she asked peering at the creature. "Don't they pretend sometimes? Isn't that where 'playing possum' comes from?"

I waved her question off, "Naw, that's just an urban legend. They don't really do that." She remained unconvinced, however, and made me take the possum to her dad, just up the road, who was an expert in all things wildlife.

Huffing in exasperation, I cinched up my too short pajama bottoms and gingerly moved the possum into the back seat of the car and started for my in-laws. Halfway there, the possum, who had indeed just been playing dead, decided to make a break for it apparently by crawling under the front seat. My first clue of this was when it stuck its cold wet nose on my ankles.

Luckily my father-in-law was able to pull my car out of the ditch with his tractor. The possum was released back into the wild and my trash was never left on the front porch again.

SUMMER NIGHTS

With daily storms, temperatures in the mid-'80s and humidity to match, I think it's safe to say that summer is here, the calendar just hasn't caught up yet. Along with summer, comes all of the obligatory summer activities; fishing, ice-cream making, and bonfires.

I'm going to make an unpopular statement here, I'm not a big fan of bonfires. They're smelly, hard to set up, and seem designed to draw in every bug in the county.

Just last week, my wife and I built a fire in our back yard, at her insistence, and spent the evening sitting around talking. She sat to one side, slowly roasting a marshmallow over the open flame, while I sat on the other, quietly smoking. Not too long before then, I had been smoldering, but a quick-thinking wife and a thrown pitcher of sweet tea had put the fire out. That'll teach me not to light a camp-fire with a gas can.

"Isn't this nice?", my wife sighed and she stared into the flames.

"Uh yeah," I said as I flicked a bug out of my burnt marshmallow before biting into it, "Much nicer than our air-conditioned house and leather sofa." I slapped at a mosquito the size of a beagle that was trying to drain me dry, "Very peaceful."

"Just think,", she said. "We could be wasting our life away in from of a T.V right now, and missing all of this."

"That sounds horrible," I pulled my flaming marshmallow from the fire, drew it close to blow it out, and promptly dropped it on my lap. "Thank goodness we didn't do that," I said, slapping at my flaming pants.

She didn't seem to pick up on my sarcasm. Don't get me wrong, I enjoy the outdoors. I just enjoy it most when I'm looking at it out of a window from inside a comfortable, climate-controlled environment. The fire was pretty, and the company I was in was unparalleled, but it was hot and muggy. The bugs seemed to have a vendetta against me personally, and my ankles kept tingling in anticipation as I imagined every poisonous snake in a mile radius being drawn to the flickering lights of the fire.

We stayed out late that night before finally dousing the fire and trudging back to the house. Smelling of burnt marshmallows, woodsmoke, and smushed bugs. I was singed and stung and my eyes smarted from the smoke that had seemed to follow me around no matter which side I sat on. All in all, I think I would have preferred a night of T.V. on the couch. But what can you do? It's tradition.

WALK THE WALK

◆ ◆ ◆

Recently, in an ill-conceived attempt to get in better shape, I decided I would take up walking. This was brought about by my dad recently completing his 5th marathon. Conversely, I recently got winded opening a pack of ramen noodles (in my defense, that plastic is almost impossible to remove)

Since my middle-aged dad could run 26 miles, I figured how hard could walking up and down my road be? So, a few weekends ago, I set off. It was in the low 80's this particular weekend and me, in my wisdom, decided I was going to walk in my cowboy boots and blue jeans.

It started off easily enough, the wind had a hint of coolness to it, birds were flitting about, singing their gay little songs, and the sky was a brilliant shade of blue. I was enjoying it so much, I decided to start singing as I walked briskly along our gravel road. I don't know if it was in criticism of my singing voice, or if he was just appalled at the sight of the fat man wearing denim walking by his house, but a neighborhood dog took offense at my presence.

Now cowboy boots aren't much good for anything but looking stylish and riding horses, and they're certainly not designed for running, but when the dog (a mix between an Irish wolfhound and a grizzly bear judging from the size of him) exploded out from under the porch, I took off. I don't know exactly how fast I ran, but I was passing cars. At one point I'm pretty sure I jumped over a slow-moving pickup, but I can't be sure, everything gets a little blurry there for a while.

Finally, somewhere around the county line, I came to a stop. I slumped to the ground, heaving out great gasps of air. Nothing in this world, I thought, was going to get me off that ground until my wife came and picked me up. About that time, a little black snake popped his head up out of the grass, curious about the trembling giant that had almost sat on him.

I shrieked and bolted again.

Several hours later, my wife pulled up beside me, laughing. "How in the world did you wind up two counties away?" she spluttered.

I didn't reply as I laid there on my back, watching the buzzards that were circling hopefully above me. Eventually, I was able to pull myself into the car without using my legs.

The next weekend I went and bought a treadmill. From now on, my walking is going to be done in front of the T.V. Although, I don't think I'll watch Animal Planet while I'm doing it.

THE DEVILS DANDRUFF

◆ ◆ ◆

The Devils Dandruff. Cottonwood cocaine. The other yellow snow. I'm talking, of course, about pollen. As soon as the weather begins to warm up, sure as death and taxes, all southerners know the yellow wave is coming.

I made a mistake after my wife and I first got married by making some smart-aleck comment (shocking I know) about her allergies. At the time I had never suffered so much as a sniffle from the yellow menace.

"It's just my superior immune system," I half boasted, half joked., "My strength is as that of ten men because my heart is pure."

My wife eyed me blearily over the tissue she had held to her nose, "You know I have access to all of your food before you eat it right?"

It's amazing how caring and considerate I became after that.

I paid for my comments just a few years later, however. One spring day my wife got home to find me laying out on the couch.

"I think I'm dying," I croaked, "My throat hurts, my eyes are watering, I'm congested," I sneezed, "And I can't stop *sneezing!* It's gotta be the flu."

She laughed and dropped her purse on the couch next to me, "It's just allergies. I have some anti-contestants in the purse, take a few and you'll be fine."

I took a few Benadryl and huddled on the couch in my misery.

My wife came back in and stopped when she saw me, "Stop it." She said.

"Stop what?" I asked stuffily.

"That's your Pondering face." She crossed her arms, "Usually when you get that look something winds up on fire."

I brightened up, "Hey that's a good id-"

"No Caleb, you are not burning the pollen in the air. I don't even know how you would *begin* to go about doing that."

"It would be easy!" I said, getting excited, "All I would need is an aerosolized-"

"No", she said firmly.

So I spent most of that spring inside, only venturing out when I absolutely had to, and only then after I was loaded up to the gills on antihistamines. Pollen season passed and everything went back to normal.

But I must admit, whenever we had a campfire that Fall, I would always leer at the trees around us right before tossing in another log. I've warred with bees and groundhogs, cats, and snakes. It's about time the tree's learned what I'm capable of.

A BRAIN ON AUTO-PILOT

◆ ◆ ◆

In today's fast-paced world, it's easy to get distracted. With worries about bills and jobs and whatever catastrophe the media is currently screaming is about to kill us all, it's just too much for the human brain to hold. So, the brain does what any good operating system does; it relegates certain activities to run on auto-pilot, thus freeing up more space to worry about things we have no control over.

We all do this; get into routines that we do without thinking about it. When we sit in a car, we buckle up. When we leave the house, we lock the door behind us. When it's time for bed, we grab a tube of toothpaste, squeeze a dollop onto our brush, and clean our teeth. Simple, repetitive actions that take up no brain space. It's a good system and one that works well, right up until the time it doesn't.

Right up until the tube of toothpaste you grab isn't a tube of toothpaste, it's a tube of hydrocortisone cream.

A normal brain would see the differently colored and sized tube lying where the toothpaste goes and think to itself 'that's not toothpaste, maybe I shouldn't scrub it all over my teeth.' A normal brain would look at the greasy white paste on the toothbrush and think 'hmm, my toothpaste normally has blue and white sparkles in it, maybe I should investigate before shoving this into my mouth.'

But a brain on auto-pilot doesn't.

On the plus side, I probably had the cleanest mouth in Pickens county for about 30 seconds. Right up until the words coming out of my mouth when I realized what I'd done would have made my mother wash my mouth out with soap if she'd have heard them.

Similarly, it's routine for me to grab my bottle of shampoo, lather up, and wash my hair. My shampoo is always in the same spot, so my brain doesn't even think when it goes to reach for the bottle. Unbeknownst to me, my wife had given our dogs a bath in the tub earlier that same day and had left their pet shampoo in the shower.

My hair was healthy and glowing for a week after that. And, as an added bonus, I know for sure now that I don't have any fleas or ticks. Other than that, I suffered no ill effects from it. Well, other than that incident with the mailman. But I'm sure he's used to being barked at, though probably not by an overweight bearded man with incredibly clean teeth and oddly flowing hair.

LAW'S CONCERNING RUDENESS

♦ ♦ ♦

Rudeness is becoming an epidemic in the country. I don't just mean the big, political, make-the-newspaper rudeness, I'm talking about small, everyday types of rudeness. Since my letters to the Governor calling for Dueling Laws to be reinstated have gone unanswered, I'd like to set my sights a little lower. Normally I'm the last person to ask for more laws or government oversight, but I think in this case it will actually enrich everyone's life.

Law #1: If you hold the door open for someone, and they walk through without saying "Thank you", it should be legal to grab that person, pull them back out the door, and shut it in their face.

Law #2: If you let somebody over on the interstate, and they don't give you the little "thank you" wave, you should be allowed to hit them with your car. Not a hard hit. Just a little tap on the bumper.

Law #3: If you smile and nod at somebody in passing and they just give you a cold look, it should be legal to trip them.

Law #4: Anyone who bumps into you in the store and doesn't say "Excuse me", should be rammed, in the ankles, with a shopping buggy.

Law #5: Tailgaters (those who drive ride against your bumper when you're driving down the road in an attempt to make you speed up) should be arrested and made to put governers on their vehicles that won't allow it to go any fast than 20 miles under the speed limit.

As helpful as these laws would be, they would only address the symptom and not the disease. I'm afraid the root cause of all the rudeness in the country seems to be from spoiled children, who grow up to be spoiled adults. To remedy this, I propose we hire an Old Man for every school.

The Old Man's sole purpose will be there to provide discipline for the children. Any bad behavior will be addressed with either a disappointed glance, a long story about how it was back in his day, or, in extreme circumstances, a belt whoopin. Good behavior will be rewarded with a fishing trip, and maybe a pocket knife.

Now there are those that say whipping children is immoral. I say bull honkey. I'm nearly 30 years old and to this day I still cringe at the sound of a belt being drawn through the loops of a pair of denim pants. If children are raised right, we could do away with police sirens and just play the sounds of a belt coming off. That'll stop bad behavior in its tracks every time.

MY BIG MOUTH

◆ ◆ ◆

From time to time my lack of tact has gotten me into trouble. What sounds innocent and kind in my head, often has a way of coming out as rude and abrasive. Understand, I have the best of intentions, I just don't always communicate them very well. Family and close friends know this about me, so they often overlook my gaffes. Strangers and people at work, however, don't understand why the big, fluffy, smiling guy is being such a jerk.

A good example; just last week a woman at work was showing pictures of her kid to everybody. The child looked pitiful, peaked and pale, with a brave little smile on her face. I saw it, grimaced and said, "I'm so sorry. She'll be in my thoughts and prayers."

Turns out, there was nothing wrong with the child. Some babies are just naturally ugly. Needless to say, the mother was not amused.

Nothing can compare to the incident that happened last year, however. In my company, we all pass around cards to sign whenever there is a big occasion for someone that works there. Birthdays, weddings, pregnancies, they all get a card. This translates into hundreds of cards a year that we all have to sign. The trick, when you have to sign little seemingly personalized little notes a dozen times a month, is to create a little template of what you're going to say, and just reuse it.

This particular month we had an abnormally high number of people retiring, I must have signed nearly 10 by the end of the month. I was very busy that day, so when a card was dropped onto my desk to sign, I didn't even glance at it. I just picked it up and wrote the same thing I had written 10 times before that same month, "Congratulations. I know you've been looking forward to this day for a long time. You deserve this." Signed my name and sent it on to the next person.

Unfortunately, however, it wasn't a retirement card. It was a sympathy card. A man at our company had lost his wife to an illness. My note was delivered, along with flower arrangement, to the funeral home. Human Resources got called in on that one and I barely kept my job. Only a long history of well-meaning, but misguided incidents in the past saved my job. Although, that man still won't speak to me.

I'm also not asked to sign any more company cards. Human Resources has deemed it "An unjustifiable liability risk." Who would have ever thought that an HR department would be so humorless? I wonder if I should mention it to them the next time I'm called in there?

TIME WASTERS

◆ ◆ ◆

It's never been easier to be alive than it is right now. Global communication happens in real-time. Supply chain and farming technology has risen to the point that even the poorest of Americans seldom have to worry about where their next meal is coming from. The lowest social class in this country enjoys a standard of living that previously even Kings could only aspire to. Within my pocket, I hold a small computer through which I can access the entire sum of all human knowledge.

I typically use it to look at Facebook.

With all that being said, I have a complaint (surprise, surprise). I am surrounded by time wasters.

Little, niggling things that seem to eat up a small portion of my day. An example: I went to get gas earlier, and slid my little card into the machine to pay. The first message that popped up was, "Is this a credit or a debit card?", first of all, this machine can access my bank, and tell if I have enough money to pay for gas by looking at my personal account. Yet it can't tell if I'm using a credit or debit card?

Fair enough, so I made my entry. The next message popped up, "Are you a rewards member?". Slightly miffed, I pressed "no." Immediately another message popped up, "See our staff to save 5% on your next purchase." Firmly I pressed, "No" again. Yet another message popped up, "Please enter your zip code."

The gas station staff found me 10 minutes later, crying and slapping at the display. They told me later that, as they carried me away, I was whimpering "I just wanted to buy gas, I just wanted to buy gas."

Unfortunately, it's like that wherever you go. I go to the grocery store and have to firmly, yet politely tell the cashier that "No I'm not a rewards member, yes I realize that it would save me money, no I don't want to sign up, yes I'm quite sure I don't want to sign up." Then when I leave, they circle the receipt and ask me to take a brief survey. I came to exchange cash for goods and/or services. I didn't come to take a test for you.

There are still several stores in Jasper that I'm not allowed back in because the staff got too insistent on offering me coupons, and I snapped.

Living has gotten easier, but it's also gotten more complicated. Instead of spending 12 hours a day in the fields, we spend 8 hours a day working, and another 8 hours dealing with little time wasters.

Sometimes I miss the fields.

A RURAL LEXICON

◆ ◆ ◆

Pickens county is growing, with new residents joining us every day. While most of them are from surrounding areas, some are from farther away. As such, it seems some of them are unfamiliar with some of our words and phrases. It's a truth that we have a language all our own in the South, so I decided to sit down and write up a brief lexicon of some of the keywords and phrases that may be confusing to some people.

Far: A flame, typically found in a grill or a campfire. Not to be mistaken for a unit of distance. (For a unit of distance, please see "yonder")

Tire: A tall building. Such as a cellphone tower or the one constructed in Babel.

Tar: The round things that a car drives on.

Warsh: To clean. Also a type of rag.

These are just a few of the words that I have noticed some people having trouble with. It's also dangerous. Heaven forbid there's a fire in a movie theater, and some good old country boys see's it and tries to warn everyone. If someone is unfamiliar with some of our words, they may sit there wondering "Why does that hillbilly keep yelling that somethings far? What does it matter the distance?" Instead of running for safety. This list could save lives!

There are also phrases that some people may be confused by if they are unfamiliar with the area, such as:

"Yeah, I need to work on that here pretty soon."- This means the work will be done anywhere from 1-3 years down the road.

"Boy, I need to work on that one of these days." – This will never get done.

"My wife kinda hinted that she wants me to fix that, but I ain't gonna let her rush me." – This will be done immediately, at least it will if the man is smart.

Now you should be able to decipher such sentences as: "I was warshing my new tars when I noticed the cellphone tire was on far." As well as many others. Another tidbit to help you acclimate to the area. We always pull to the side of the road when a funeral procession drives by, even if we don't know the deceased. If you're wearing a hat, you'll be expected to remove it until the procession is passed.

Also, in the event of a death, you will be expected to bring a casserole. It doesn't matter what kind, but it will fit in with the 40 other casserole dishes already at the funeral home.

I hope this helps any new residents, and welcome to the county.

PLAY IT AGAIN, SAM

◆ ◆ ◆

My friends have always had a hard time understanding how I can watch the same old movies over and over again. "It's a good movie", they'll say "But you just watched it last month. Doesn't it get boring to you?"

And the answer is no, I enjoy them just as much the 20th time as I did the first time. It seems like I'm in the minority on this one, but I love rewatching my favorites. I pondered on that, and the only answer I could come up with is that it's comforting to me.

In the real world, we're so often beset with trouble and the uncertainty of how it will resolve. We're left in the dark, wandering blindly from trial to trial sometimes it seems. But in those old movies, I begin the story with the comfort of knowing how it will end. I know that the heroes will bravely face hard times as they come. There will be bold ideals that they hold too. Ideals that they are willing to give up their lives for, ideals that hold high for others to see. There will be beautiful, eloquent speeches that make your' blood boil with vigor and songs that set your heart ablaze.

The small, overmatched heroes will stand in the face of an unbeatable foe, and come out the other side unscathed. Then they'll return at the end of the story to green lands, back to the comfort of their own cozy homes. The screen will fade to black with our heroes in their prime, laughing and looking to the future and all that it holds for them, and that's how they'll always be in our minds; young and victorious, with clear skies ahead.

Those movies show us the very best of what we would like life to be, and so often isn't. The good guys live happily ever after, and the villain is always defeated. A pure heart carries you through the worst adversity, and a noble ideal is enough to stand against the fiercest of foes. It's comforting to me to watch that, and for a while, I get to live in that world.

It's escapism, plain and simple. For a while, I get to escape when this world seems too big and overpowering. Then after the movie ends I'll look around, and a little of their courage seems to have transferred to me, and the world doesn't seem so dark anymore. Don't get me wrong, I love my life. I love this world that I have been fortunate enough to be born into. But sometimes it's nice to know how the story will end.

THE DRIVING REPORT

◆ ◆ ◆

It is my observation that on highway 515 there are two different speeds:40 miles per hour, and 90. There is no middle ground. The drive to Canton, from highway 53, takes between 10 minutes and 50, depending on which lane you're in.

I figured this out after countless trips to work, and finding myself in the right-hand lane, stuck behind one of the aforementioned 40 miles per hour drivers. I found that I couldn't move over to the left lane, and pass them, because of the 90 miles per hour drivers. Trying to change lanes in these circumstances is almost impossible, requiring precise timing and a steady hand.

Since I possess neither, I'm typically stuck in the right lane until my exit.

I've also noticed that drivers are increasingly aggressive of late. While I wholeheartedly support moving into the right lane unless you're passing someone, I can't understand why people want to ride right on your bumper when you're going the speed limit (or perhaps a little faster).

I will say that these drivers are usually pretty friendly though. Many times I've noticed them in my rearview window, waving animatedly at me as we putter along at 5 miles over the posted speed limit. I can't guarantee they were using all of their fingers while they were waving, but then, you can't have everything I suppose.

Road conditions are watched pretty closely by drivers on our fair highway I have noticed. When conditions are dry and clear, half the drivers fly along at speeds approaching 90, veering among traffic with no regards to safe braking distance, or indicator lights. When conditions are wet or icy, I'm pleased to report that they typically slow to a more sedate 85 miles per hour, and sometimes use their blinkers. Occasionally. By accident.

All in all, I like to think that these people are just trying to do their civic duty. Unsure of how to donate to local law enforcement, they have elected to make their donations by paying traffic tickets. Scarcely a morning goes by without my seeing someone pulled over, blue lights flashing. It does the heart good to see such civic-mindedness in our community.

Other drivers see, to support this attitude by brazenly speeding as they pass these individuals. Perhaps a little envious that they didn't get to make their contribution to the county this time.

Either way, I am happy to report that the highways are completely safe to drive on. Assuming you are comfortable driving 90 miles an hour. Or 40. The real dangers are those nutjobs (of which I am a member) that insist on going the speed limit.

NO CAUSE FOR ALARM

◆ ◆ ◆

From time to time my wife has accused me of being...colorful in my writing of my adventures. I'm not quite sure what she means by this as I have held myself to the strictest of journalistic standards as I have attempted to chronicle some of my more entertaining misadventures. That being said, I feel I need to stress that every word that you are about to read is entirely true. There have been no exaggerations or embellishments because frankly, this story doesn't need any.

Let me tell you the story of what happened when Corporate came to town.

Where I work, corporate is division who's name is spoken about in fearful, reverent whispers. The smart employees try to schedule their vacation days around Corporates visits. This last week, however, it was an "All hands on deck" situation. We were told in no uncertain terms that management expected us all to be there to roll out the red carpet.

On the day they arrived, I combed my hair, trimmed my beard, and wore my best Sunday-go-to-meeting clothes. It went well. They made a brief speech, then retired to the conference room with our head guy, Jethro. To set the stage, you need to know that the conference room is located about 10 feet from the front door. I was parked 5 feet from the front door.

Tired of smiling and trying to seem agreeable, I retired to my car for my lunch break. I forgot my keys at my desk so I unlocked the car with an app on my phone and sat in my car to enjoy the silence. In the end, I reluctantly plastered a smile back on my face and climbed out of my car.

Now my car has a security measure. If it's unlocked from my phone and then locked from inside, you have to unlock it from your phone again in order to get out. I neglected that step. As soon as I got out of my car, it started beeping softly, letting me know I had 10 seconds to hit the appropriate button on my phone to stop the alarm. I whipped my phone out, and the phone went black as it crashed.

An ear-shattering wail went up from my car. It was so loud, it set off the alarms of the cars on either side. Frantically I slapped at my phone as it slowly rebooted. For 5 minutes I stood in the pouring rain, cursing at the block of plastic in my hand as I maniacally slapped at the screen. Finally, the alarm shut off. I slowly looked up to see HR, Jethro, and half of the corporate delegation with their heads poked out of the door, all staring at me. Jethro was grinning ear to ear, and I knew that I would never live this down.

HOLIDAY BRAIN

◆ ◆ ◆

I have to admit, with the recent holidays I have been suffering a severe case of "Holiday Brain". What with long weekends, days off work in the middle of the week, and vacation time I've taken at the last minute, I really couldn't tell you what day of the week it was without consulting a calendar and my phone first.

So when I woke up the other day and glanced at the clock, I wasn't surprised that I had neglected to set my alarm the night before and was now running 30 minutes late for work. I jumped out of bed and hurriedly began to dress in the dark. I always try to avoid turning the lights on when I get ready for work in the morning because I don't like to wake my wife up. This morning, however, I didn't have the benefit of clothes laid out neatly the night before, so I rummaged through my dresser like a raccoon in the garbage can.

It got interesting at one point when I tried to put my socks and shirt on at the same time, resulting in my bouncing between dressers and the bed like an overweight pinball, frantically trying to balance on one leg and simultaneously trying to keep my curses quiet enough to not wake my wife. About this time I found a lego that my nephew had left when he had visited during the holidays, luckily I had a mouthful of undershirt at the time, so my shriek of pain was muffled.

I stumbled out the front door 5 minutes later, wearing wrinkled dress pants and an inside out button-up shirt. Glancing down I noticed I was wearing a tennis shoe on one foot, black dress shoe on the other. I didn't have time to correct the error though, so I jumped in the car and pulled up to our new gate. I sat, bouncing up and down to vent excess adrenaline as the gate slowly crept open. The gate opener was new, I had just installed in the day before. I screamed in frustration as I ground to a halt, only halfway open.

I lept from the car and wrestled it wide enough for my car to inch through, sliding in mud in the process and winding up on my butt. Doggedly I climbed back into the car and tore out of my driveway.

I careened into the parking lot of work, 45 minutes past when I should have been there. Panting I raced up to the door and tried jerking it open. Locked. Blearily I looked from the door to the parking lot, noticing for the first time that mine was the only car in it. Slowly I pulled out my phone and saw on the screen "Sunday, January 6th ".

NO OFFENSE, BUT...

◆ ◆ ◆

What to write about this week? In today's world, it's getting harder and harder to write humor columns. Everyones so darn offended all the time. In last week's article, I somehow managed to offend football lovers, mountain lion lovers, and goat lovers.

(I've been told that calling someone a "goat-lover" is offensive. The proper term is "Goat enthusiast"? Somehow that doesn't seem much better. Next time you get into an argument with someone, tell them that they are "Enthused by goats". I don't think that will go over well.)

My point is that you can't write anything these days without some sort of special interest group getting in an uproar about it. Maybe I should just write advice columns. Dispensing sage, simple advice on how to deal with everyday problems. That probably wouldn't work out either. Most likely yo have to be licensed, insured, and part of some sort of union in order to give people advice.

I miss the old days when gruff advice was dispensed by grizzled old men. I can picture that in today's world:

Dear. Gruff Gus,

I've been out of work for a while now because I can't find a job that *feels* right for me. I've had offers but they weren't socially progressive enough. My parents are on my case because I haven't contributed in two years. How do I get them off my back? Signed, Marvin the Millennial.

Marvin,

Get a job and quit yer whining.

Signed Gus.

Gus would be publicly shamed and probably sued nowadays. But I think that's the problem now. People think if you disagree with them, or correct them, then they have a right to make you agree with them just because they're offended.

It's hard to grow and improve yourself if you're not corrected or told when you're doing wrong. People are told they are perfect the way they are. I'll share a secret with you; no one is perfect the way they are. Diamonds aren't perfect when they're mined. They're rough, dirty, ugly pieces of rock. It's not until they're shaped, and smoothed that they can truly shine. People now don't want to be smoothed, they want to be told they're fine in their original state.

I didn't mean to sit down and write a diatribe on the state of the world. I was going to sit down and write a humorous article on my second run-in with our resident possum (natures whack-a-mole) but shoot, that would probably offend possum lovers. (I'm being told calling someone a "possum-lover" is just as offensive as calling them a "goat-lover", jeez you just can't win)

THE LONGEST DAY

◆ ◆ ◆

As most of you know, my wife has to put up with a lot being married to me. So whenever the opportunity arises for me to do something for her, I typically leap at the chance.

Last year she asked me if I wanted to go Black Friday shopping with her. Now, like most guys, I treat shopping like a military operation. I identify my target, for the sake of argument lets' say a new pack of undershirt, I chart its location, and I note the quickest means of obtaining the target and exiting the combat zone. I like to get in, get the item, and get out.

Needless to say, an entire day spent randomly shopping for Christmas presents ranked right up there next to an un-anesthetized root canal. But since I had recently just set fire to her favorite rhododendron bush (a casualty in my war on the yellow jackets) I couldn't really in good conscious turn her down.

Let me start by saying I feel like I'm a pretty tough guy. I've broken bones (all my own), I've suffered cuts and bruises and lacerations, and I've seen every Quenton Tarontino film. I thought I had seen some pretty serious stuff before. None of this prepared me for the horror of what I saw that day. "This isn't too bad" I thought standing in an orderly line later that night.

Inside the store, I could see a group of employees in a huddle, it looked like they were playing "Rock, Paper, Scissors". The loser, a scrawny teenager, started walking towards the doors while the others backed away rapidly, looks of relief on their faces. He timidly approached the locked doors, while the crowd, who up to this point had been rather pleasant, stirred restlessly. He reached up one trembling hand, unlocked the doors, turned and ran.

I was puzzled at first, then the crowd gave a great surge, and started pouring into the store. I was swept away from my wife in the early minutes as all those pleasant faced women transformed in front of my eyes. Gone were the gentle smiles and good natured jokes. In it's place was a ravening horde, with only one thought on it's mind, "getting the best deal".

I met up with my wife a short time later, nursing a rapidly blackening eye given to me by a sweet old lady that decided I was in the way.

"Are we about done here?" I asked her in a shaky voice.

She looked up at me, a vibrant smile on her face, "Sure! Ready for the next store?" I stifled a sob as I trailed after her bobbing red head in the churning crowd.

MOW MONEY, MOW PROBLEMS

◆ ◆ ◆

Long time readers will remember the saga of the lawnmower. To those that are newer (or don't care enough about my piddly problems to remember) last year, I had a multi-month repair project underway to repair my old riding mower. The story ended with me finally getting the mower running but, unbeknownst to me, that story had a 'to be continued' at the end.

All this to say; my mower has died again. Kaput. The end. No amount of elbow grease, duct tape, or shouted profanities were enough to coax it back to life this time. This left me with the unenviable task of buying a new one.

"How much can they cost, 3 or 4 hundred dollars?" I mused as I went to check out what the local store had to offer. My wife had to wheel me out in a shopping cart when I saw the asking price. My first car didn't cost as much as the barest model they offered, so it was back to the drawing board.

After my wife nixed my idea to rope a line of weedeaters to the front of my truck, I finally settled on hiring someone to cut my grass. Luckily, I have a friend that cuts grass, so I was able to get something on the books for just a few days later.

Now I won't put too fine of a point on it, I'm a redneck. I replace my own oil, fix my own appliances, and mow my own grass. Always have and swore I always would, so to hire someone to cut my grass when I am an able-bodied, red-blooded American, went against the grain.

That lasted about five minutes after watching my friend zip through my yard, doing in minutes what used to take me hours (once you factored in jumping off my mower and stopping every few minutes to replace the belt that insisted on falling out.)

I'll admit, I got a bit smug as I watched him sweat in the summer heat. I even went and got a cup of ice-cream to enjoy as I watched him. The grass hadn't been mown in the better part of a month at this point, so he had his work cut out for him.

Eventually, I made it out to the front porch where I propped my feet up to enjoy the show and my ice-cream.

My friend swears what happened next was purely accidental, a mixture of an anemic garden coupled with an overgrown yard, but I still think it was deliberate. Possibly payback for my mocking saluting him with a spoonful of Moosetracks.

On his next turn around the yard, he flew through a quarter of my garden, instantly mulching carrots, lettuce, and tomato plants. Months of hard work down the drain in seconds.

The next day I bought my own mower.

PUTTING ON AIRS

◆ ◆ ◆

Sometimes the smallest of actions can have wide-reaching repercussions. The smallest twitch, the tiniest movement, can send your life on a downward spiral, and you won't know what action will cause it until it happens. It's an unavoidable, immutable truth of life. Such a thing happened to me last weekend when I killed my air conditioner.

Summer was in her death throws, lashing out with one last heat wave because she finally succumbed to fall. The thermostat read 93 and I, in a rare act of motivation, decided I would tend to the yard. When I got to the air conditioner, I noticed that the weeds had grown up around it pretty badly. Instead of dealing with my ever-troublesome weedeater, I decided I would use my sling blade to clear the growth. I recited lines from the Billy-Bob Thornton movie as I worked.

"Mmm-hmmm," I grunted as I swung the blade, "French fried taters." So caught up was I in my acting, I wasn't paying attention to what I was doing as closely as I should have. I let the sling-blade get too close to the unit. One-quarter inch too far. I felt the clang of metal on metal, heard the hiss of escaping Freon, and my friend died.

I loved that air conditioner. Many's the day we spent in each other's company. Me, lying on the couch in my pajamas, it humming along in the background, merrily doing its job. We were like family, and I killed him.

My wife was uncharacteristically kind about the whole ordeal when I told her.

"Oh, great job genius." She said, "Real smart."

"Uh, thanks," I said, unused to her being that supportive. Despite my loss, I didn't have time to grieve. The thermometer was still climbing and the weatherman was calling for even warmer temperatures the following week. A few phone calls later and I had a replacement on its way for only slightly more than my entire house had cost me.

I stood there a few days later, weeping, as they hauled my old friend away. Silent tears flowed down my face to mingle with the sweat. Nobody noticed.

After the repair guys left, I slowly approached the stranger attached to the back of my house. We eyed each other warily for a few minutes. I patted it gently, then went inside to stand in front of the thermostat. Slowly I reached up and pressed the button to activate the new air-conditioner. It rumbled to life. The sound was different, the background murmur wasn't that of my old friend. But as the cool, dry air began to pour from the vents, I smiled a little. I think we're going to get along just fine.

BIG ROCK DANDY MOUNTAINS

◆ ◆ ◆

Soon the people of Pickens and surrounding counties will gather to celebrate our most sacred of local festivals. A festival that has been passed down through the generations of our forefathers until this present day. A time-honored tradition, a celebration of Pickens County and all that it stands for. I speak, of course, about Marblefest.

A quick Wikipedia search will tell you a lot about Marblefest. It will tell you that it was founded way back in the far off distant year of 1980. It will tell you where it's located (Jasper, Ga) and will tell you when it's running (October 5th-6th). But it won't tell you everything. It won't tell you *why* it was founded, and without knowing the why, we lose the heart of the thing itself.

As previously stated, Marblefest was founded in 1980, Ronald Reagan had just been elected, Whip It was at the top of the billboard charts, and bell-bottoms were still considered the height of fashion. Unbeknownst to the rest of the busy world, in a small little mountain town in North Georgia, two men were plotting.

Although their names have been lost to the misty recesses of time, their conversation was penned down for posterity. It went as follows:

Man A: "We have to come up with something to get people in town. Something that will really draw them in. What do you think will work?"

Man B: "Some sort of festival. People love festivals. Something that can compete with Blairsville and Ellijay."

Man A: "What do we have that can compete with apple pie and moonshine?"

The record shows that both men stared at the ground, deep in thought. One of them kicked a rock pensively then his eyes lit up. Excitedly he bent down and grabbed the stone, holding it up for the other man to see.

Man A: "This! We can go show people where 90% of the cold, dense edifices in Washington come from!"

Man B scratched his head: "I didn't know there were any congressman from Pickens."

Man A resisted the urge to throw the rock at Man B: "No dummy, marble! We can have a Marble Festival! We supply 90% of the marble in all the buildings and monuments in D.C.!"

Man B perked up as he caught on: "Hey that's a great idea! People love rocks. We can even come up with a slogan. Something like, 'If you love watching paint dry, you'll love this.' "

The two men spent the rest of the day hashing out the details (and improving on the slogan) and Marblefest was born. So come join us in the First Mountain City as we celebrate our heritage with food, fun, and games. Come enjoy our local delicacies, listen to our musicians, and (of course) our marble.

BIG CITY BLUES

◆ ◆ ◆

Progress is inevitable. Technology advances daily, and what was once thought to be impossible, is now commonplace. Man is inexorably drawn to new heights, to reach the unattainable. It's in our nature, it's who we are as a species. This is usually a good thing, sometimes, however, we are the victims of our own progress. I am one such person.

Not very long ago, the county came and paved our road, and I am devastated. It happened without warning, I came home from work one day to find my beloved, dusty, potholed piece of Georgia topography gone, vanished beneath a layer of steaming blacktop. I called to complain, to get them to remove the monstrosity in front of my house, but they were less than understanding.

The lady I spoke to with the county tried to defend their actions. She kept saying how much smoother my ride would be, how much less dust would be kicked up. Why, she even tried to say how thankful I should be that I could finally keep a clean car! She didn't seem to understand that these were all the reasons I didn't want to do away with the dirt road in the first place.

I need that bumpy road first thing in the morning. City folks drink a cup of coffee to wake them up on their ride to work, but we in the South have a better method. Anyone who lives on a dirt road can attest to the fact that hitting a pothole the size of a cow when you're racing around a bend, late to work, does more to wake you up than a whole pot of coffee!

I like the dust it kicks up too. A clean car is a mark of shame in the south, it smacks of putting on airs. Also, without dust, how else am I supposed to know if someones coming to visit? Before the road was paved, we could tell if we were having company a good half hour before they got here. My wife and I would be sitting on the porch, drinking a glass of sweet tea, when we would see a dust trail in the distance.

"Looks like your folks are coming to visit." I would say.

"Yep, you better go put a pair of pants on." She would reply.

"Nah, I got another 20 minutes before they get here. I'll finish my glass."

Now, when we have visitors, it's a surprise. I'm going to have to ask people to start calling first. That or start wearing pants around the house all the time, which I refuse to do.

If I wanted to worry about being presentable all the time, I'd move to the big city. Somewhere like Canton.

THE REAL GHOST HUNTERS OF PICKENS COUNTY

◆ ◆ ◆

I've always been skeptical of ghost hunting shows on TV. Beyond my own disbelief in the supernatural, I find it hard to believe that a TV crew and a few excitable reality stars are able to consistently find evidence of ghosts, week after week, on their show, yet still walk away without consensus amongst the scientific community.

Well, perhaps "evidence" is too strong of a word. I tuned into an episode late the other night just in time to catch this example of quality TV.

"I'm looking for any spirits that may inhabit this creepy old insane asylum we're staying in tonight," The host said. The floor creaked slightly.

"Oh so your name is Todd and you died in 1946 from tuberculosis, that's amazing!" Then the crew fist-bumped and declared the building "super haunted".

I've always thought it was all made up.

So the other night I decided to do a little ghost hunting of my own. On the way home from celebrating my wife's birthday, I decided to pull into a local cemetery and see what if we could "communicate with the spirits". My wife was not as impressed with the idea as I was, it being her special day and all, but when I explained what I was trying to do, she warmed up to the idea.

"Oh just in time for Halloween too. This will be fun!"

I'll admit, the silent cemetery, lit only by the half-moon overhead, was a bit creepy, and I began to regret my decision to try this. With trembling hands, I pulled out my phone and began recording, "Are there any ghosts here?" I squeaked. The only reply was a whisper of wind across the car.

We sat in silence, listening. Just then the wind picked up slightly, and a branch screeched suddenly against the side of the car. An unearthly screech filled the air.

Later I laughed about it as we drove down the road, the sound of the wind loud through the sunroof. "I can't believe people think that's creepy. Shoot, looking out over the cemetery like that was downright peaceful."

"Speak up," My wife said, "I can't hear you over the hole in the roof."

"It's not a hole," I said, rubbing my sore head, "It's the sunroof."

"Whatever," She said, crossing her arms and leaning back into her seat, "We didn't start out the evening with a head shaped hole in the roof. And your unearthly screech about half deafened me. Although," She cocked her head to the side and started to laugh, "It was funny watching you try to drive us out of there for 10 minutes before realizing you hadn't even cranked the car back up."

ALL I HEAR IS BANJOS

◆ ◆ ◆

Living in the South comes with a lot of baggage. People have a lot of preconceived notions about you the second you open your mouth, and that slow southern drawl starts coming out. As soon as you start dropping your consonants and lengthening your vowels, they automatically assume you rooted for the crazed rednecks in Deliverance. Which is just absurd. I mean I *understand* where the rednecks were coming from, what with having those intruders just show up on their land like that. That doesn't mean I don't think they overreacted a bit.

Let's just admit that both sides were in the wrong and move on.

And that sure was some good banjo playing.

Something about a banjo just typifies the South to me. Something about the notes, ugly when played by themselves with their off-kilter twang, but when played together it somehow solidifies into a harmonious whole. That's how Southern life is, when viewed piecemeal, it doesn't look too appealing. But as soon as it's all strung together, it's a thing of beauty.

People laugh at broken down cars in a yard, but beyond the walls of the house just beyond, is a hard-working father who goes out every evening and works on getting at least one of them running so the family will have a second car. Dirt roads seem primitive and poor to most, but there's a certain beauty that just can't be denied in those red Georgia clay trails.

Our pace may seem slow to the rest of the world, maddening to some in our fast-paced society. But within those slow, friendly interactions among small-town folks, is the knowledge that life is more than just getting between point A and point B. Life is what happens in between those destinations. It's in the passing wave to the lonely old man sitting on his porch, or the friendly handshake with someone you only see at church on the weekends. It's in a couple sitting on their front porch, watching their grandchildren joyously leaping and jumping, capturing fireflies in an old mason jar.

I won't even try to defend our food, biscuits and gravy speak for themselves and they don't need any help from me.

To most of the world, the South is an appalling place. They see it as being filled with slow people, with even slower minds. They see an ugly patchwork of mismatched parts and all that may be true. But we're more than the sum of our parts, and in our multitude of parts, there is beauty. The South has its problems, just like anywhere else, but to me? All I hear is banjos.

AFTERWORD

I want to thank each and every one of you for taking time to read. It's been a fun ride, so thank you for making this possible. A new Simple Man book will be coming in the future.

In the mean time, if you like Ghost's and Ghoulie's and spookiness, check out some of my other books. The links are on the next back.

Also, jump over to my website for news updates and giveaways. www.caleb-smith.net

BOOKS BY THIS AUTHOR

Discord's Shadow

Accused of a murder he didn't commit. A looming threat from the ancient past. One ageless assassin. A countdown to execution. And snark. Lots and lots of snark.

Nate Silver has a history. A history he would rather forget.

After centuries of bloodshed and war, he just wants to be left alone to run his janitorial service for the supernatural. It's a step down for the former warrior, but it's the peaceful life he's always craved. After an enforcer for the reigning body of the supernatural world is killed in front of him, however, Nate is pulled headlong back into the life he's fought so hard to leave behind.
Accused of a murder he didn't commit, and with the clock ticking down towards his own execution, Nate is left with only days to find the killer. Along with his werewolf partner, Dan, Nate will have to comb through the mystic underbelly of the city of Atlanta in search of answers.

As the dead begin to pile up, however, a darker threat is discovered. One that indicates the murder wasn't as random as it first appeared.

And if all the werewolves, vampires, trolls (not to mention one disturbingly insightful snake lady) aren't enough, there's a new player on the field. One possibly older than Christianity itself.

And he's gunning for Nate.

Errant Son

I took a deep breath, "You make a tempting offer." I said thought-
fully. I sighed heavily; the decision made.
She nodded, a small triumphant smile on her face.
I smiled back.
Then I blew her out the window.

Nate Silver has been shot at, blown up, beaten, and kidnapped, all
within the space of a few days.

Now he's just ready for a return to his simple life where his biggest
worry was whether or not he'd make rent this month.
When an old friend shows up on his doorstep, however, bloodied
and on the run, Nate knows that he has to get involved.

Risking execution, he breaks his parole and heads off to the North
Georgia mountains in search of answers.

While there, he runs into a familiar face who persuades him to
help track down a little girl that's gone missing. On the trail, Nate
is faced with a threat greater than any he's encountered before. An
ancient race of beings that have no business walking the earth are
back.

And they're pissed.

Nate will have to use every bit of cunning, and more luck than he's
owed, just to make it out alive.

And there's still the little matter of making rent this month.

Fallen State

Without sparing the man at my feet another glance, I slowly turned. As the tumult died down, people began to peak their heads out from shelter, phones still raised as they recorded the battle. My shirt, almost completely consumed by fire at this point, fell away from me as I took a faltering step forward.

"I think," I rasped, my voice raw, "I think I screwed up."

Then I collapsed to the street.

Darkness falls.

An ancient evil, long buried, has awoken. Betrayed and imprisoned for millennia, he once again roams the Earth, and he only has one thought on his mind.

Destruction.

And he wants Nate to help him.

Faced with an overwhelmingly powerful foe, Nate is presented with an impossible choice; either join or die.

He'll have to choose between the organization that has oppressed the supernatural world with their iron fist for centuries, and the being that has taken away everything he's ever cared about.

Whichever side he chooses, the other will want him dead.

Either way, at least now he won't have to worry about rent.

Ponderings Of A Simple Man

This compilation of articles by award-winning columnist Caleb Smith, "Ponderings of a Simple Man" will make you laugh out loud with every page. Filled with 66 "best-of" articles, each is a new entry in the ongoing battle between a man and his own bumbling incompetence. Supported by his kind and long-suffering wife, the Simple Man faces challenges in home repair, malicious household pets, and all the various flora and fauna north Georgia has to offer. Learn the motivating properties of a swarm of wasps, why it's a bad idea to use fire to deal with yellowjackets, and how difficult it is for a fat guy covered in oil to chase a cat up a tree, along with much, much more. Filled with riotous, clean humor, "Ponderings of a Simple Man" is a collection of stories for the whole family. Join the Simple Man and his (mostly true) misadventures. He's a modern-day mountain man that just can't seem to get the hang of it.

ABOUT THE AUTHOR

Caleb Smith

Caleb Smith began reading in earnest at age 8 during a school-wide reading contest. What started out as nothing more than competition, quickly developed into a deep love of the art.

Through the years he developed a wide array of tastes; from thriller and horror, to Sci-Fi and Urban Fantasy. Eventually he grew tired of waiting for his next favorite book to be released, so he decided to start writing them himself.

He quickly learned that it was harder than it looked.

Caleb is a nerd of the highest order and will happily debate the merits of which "Star" franchise is better for hours. He lives on the side of a mountain in an undisclosed location with his wife and their boss, a 4 pound Yorkie